Charles Campbell

Some materials to serve for a brief memoir of John Daly Burk

Burk

Author of a History of Virginia

Charles Campbell

Some materials to serve for a brief memoir of John Daly Burk
Author of a History of Virginia

ISBN/EAN: 9783337281144

Printed in Europe, USA, Canada, Australia, Japan

Cover: Foto ©Raphael Reischuk / pixelio.de

More available books at **www.hansebooks.com**

SOME MATERIALS

TO

SERVE FOR A BRIEF MEMOIR

OF

JOHN DALY BURK,

AUTHOR OF A HISTORY OF VIRGINIA.

WITH A

SKETCH OF THE LIFE AND CHARACTER OF HIS ONLY CHILD,

JUDGE JOHN JUNIUS BURK.

EDITED BY

CHARLES CAMPBELL.

ALBANY, N. Y.:

JOEL MUNSELL.

1868.

PREFACE.

When Burk undertook to write a *History of Virginia*, such a work was a desideratum. There were then several histories of detached periods, but there was no one comprehensive history of the state. There were in existence many valuable historical documents and materials, which as yet had lain unnoticed and neglected. The time when Burk undertook the task was opportune : the country had now recovered, in great measure, from the calamities of the revolutionary war, and its exasperations had subsided, and many readers now had both leisure and inclination to take a more deliberate retrospect of the past. It was time that there should be written a history of the state, which had given birth to Henry and Lewis, and Nelson and Mason, and Jefferson and Madison, and the Lees and Washington.

Smith's *General History* is the ground work of all succeeding histories of Virginia, as his map is the prototype of all succeeding maps of Virginia. The second and sixth books of his history were composed by Smith himself; the third was compiled by the Rev. William Simons, doctor of divinity, and the rest of the work by Smith, from the letters and journals of about thirty different writers.

The Rev. William Stith, a native of Virginia, married a sister of Sir John Randolph, and was some time president of William and Mary College. He composed his *History of*

Virginia, at Varina, on the James river. It was published in 1747, and entitled *A History of the Discovery and Settlement of Virginia, to the year* 1624. He was a classical scholar, a true patriot, and a most faithful chronicler. His work is, in the main, a digest of the miscellaneous documents published by Smith, to which is added an account of the proceedings of the London company, in the management of the colony. It is a subject of regret, that this honest, accurate and judicious historian did not receive encouragement enough, to induce him to complete his excellent work down to his own times. He died in 1755.

Robert Beverley was born in Virginia, and educated in England.[1] The first edition of his *History of Virginia*, was published at London, in 1705, and in the same year an edition was issued at Amsterdam. The second English edition was published at London, in 1722. It differs but little from the first. The first book, the civil history of the colony, is brief, partisan and unsatisfactory, yet, perhaps, was sufficient to gratify the curiosity of the readers of that day. The second book, which treats of the natural history and productions of Virginia, is full, but deals no little in panegyric, as is usual with colonists, whose imagination is excited by the striking phenomena of a new region, and who, possessing vast tracts of uncultivated land, desire to attract immigrants to their country. The third book gives a full and minute account of the manners and customs of the Indians, and is illustrated by Gribelin's engravings. The fourth book gives a satisfactory account of the state and condition of Virginia, for which the author was very competent, having been long conversant with the records of the colony.

_____

[1] He married Ursula, daughter of William Byrd of Westover.

Sir William Keith, a governor of Pennsylvania, was a cotemporary of Spotswood, governor of Virginia. His work is entitled: *The History of the British Plantations in America. Part I. Containing the History of Virginia, with Remarks on the Trade and Commerce of that Colony.* From this it appears, that he intended to compile a series of colonial histories, but that of Virginia is the only one which he actually published. It was published at London, in 1738. He brings the narrative down to 1723, the close of Spotswood's administration. His style is good; his matter is drawn almost entirely from Stith and Beverley.

Besides Smith, Stith, Beverley and Keith, Burk, in his first volume, made use of the *Records of the London Company*, which *he* says, fell into his hands by accident, but Hening says that they were lent to him by John Randolph of Roanoke, to whom they belonged. Burk's first volume comprises a period of eighteen years, ending with the dissolution of the London company, in 1624.

His second volume closes in 1710. The principal authorities referred to in it, are Beverley, and certain manuscript records, originally compiled by Hickman, clerk in the office of the secretary of the colony, for the use of Sir John Randolph, who, at one time, meditated writing a history of Virginia, which purpose, however, he did not carry into execution.

The Hickman manuscripts were subsequently made use of by Hening, in the compilation of *The Statutes at Large of Virginia.*[1] Burk had also in his possession Colonel Byrd's *Journal*, in a manuscript volume. He does not appear to have had access to Chalmers's *Political Annals*

---

[1] See article by William Green, Esq., on Stith's *History of Virginia*, in *Southern Literary Messenger*, September, 1863.

a rare and valuable authority, published in one folio volume, in 1782.

In his third volume, Burk cites but few authorities, and his narrative gradually widens into a history of the thirteen colonies, rather than of Virginia alone. However, the revolutionary story was abruptly interrupted by his premature death, and comes down no farther than to the year 1775.

Petersburg, Va., January 4, 1868.

INTRODUCTION.

In October, 1866, William Green, Esq. of Richmond, Va., communicated to me some memoranda, which he had made with a view to the preparation of a memoir of John D. Burk, author of a *History of Virginia*, requesting, that I should combine his communications with such other facts as might be in my possession, or might be accessible to me, and prepare them for the press. I undertook the task, but rather reluctantly, as the facts regarding Burk, in my possession. were but few and meagre, and I much preferred that Mr. Green should himself go on to execute the plan which he had originated.

Recollecting, some time afterwards, my having heard that Judge Burk, the only child of John D. Burk, was still surviving, in Louisiana, I wrote to make inquiry respecting him, and learned that the judge had died in 1866, at Baton Rouge, leaving a widow, several daughters, and a son. I addressed a letter to one of the daughters, Miss Junia A. Burk, made known to her my design, and requested her to communicate to me any information that might be in her possession, regarding her grandfather. She complied with my request, in the most attentive and obliging manner, and this, although, during our correspondence, she suffered another bereavement, in the loss of her mother, whereby she was involved in increased domestic cares. I have published her communications in the form in which they were received, my design being, not to prepare a memoir, but only to collect some materials for one. Indeed, her letters were so well expressed, though written with a running pen, that I could hardly have altered their phraseology without impairing their interest.

Some account of Judge Burk appearing to appertain properly to the subject, I made some inquiries of Miss Burk in regard to her father. Her replies, on this head, will be found not the least interesting part of her communications.

C. C.

JOHN DALY BURK.

Copy of a letter from Miss Junia A. Burk.

BATON ROUGE, *August* 2, 1867.

MR. CAMPBELL,

Sir: Yours of July 19, came duly to hand, and I make it a pious duty, as well as a pleasure, to afford you all information in my power respecting my much beloved ancestor, John D. Burk. I have some few facts relative to his private life, but they are very disconnected, and I fear will be of little use to you, unless you are already in possession of dates, which may connect the limited knowledge of the circumstances of his private life, now in my possession. The short episode, which I am able to detail to you, I have often heard from my late father's own lips, who ever entertained a lively remembrance of and sincere regret for his father.

John Daly Burk was a native of Ireland, born of respectable parents, claiming descent

2

from an ancient family of the country, of the house of Clanricarde. While very young, he was placed at Trinity College, Dublin, by an uncle (whether by the father, or mother's side, is not known), and there remained until he was eighteen years of age, when he contracted a private marriage with a lady of quality, by whom he had one son. Of the final destiny of this lady and her child, nothing was known to my father; but it is to be inferred, that they died, as the subject of the following sketch afterwards married, in Virginia, the widow Curtis,[1] *nce* Borne. Under these circumstances, while holding secret intercourse with his wife, he also became connected with the secret political cabals then so ardently and enthusiastically entered

---

[1] She had two sons, Henry and Benjamin. Henry was a physician, and married a sister of John Tyler, sometime president of the United States. Dr. Curtis settled at Hanover town, in Hanover county, Va., about the year 1818, and practiced medicine in that county, for near half a century. He was a man of talents, of cultivated mind and estimable disposition, and remarkable for his decision of character. He had a son named Tyler: another son, Armistead, is now living in the vicinity of Richmond, Va.

Benjamin Curtis, brother of Henry, was a lawyer at Petersburg, in 1808.

into by the Irish gentlemen of the day, and continued in connection with the proscribed party until the untimely discovery of their plans forced him to fly the country.

The circumstance which obliged him to fly was an attempted rescue of a rebel while being led to execution, which, at the instigation of Burk,' backed by twenty-nine others, young gentlemen, who were sitting on the steps of Trinity at the time, was very nearly accomplished, when the police came up and dispersed them. Burk being a commoner, and already in disrepute with the party in power, was forced to fly for his life; and being hotly pursued by the police, escaped through a bookseller's shop, where his dog kept them at bay until he was supplied with woman's apparel by one of the inmates of the house, a Miss Daly (which, by the way, is the only reason for his bearing that name, as he afterwards retained it through a romantic sense of gratitude towards the person who rendered him this service). Escaping from thence, he got on board of a ship then in port, and bound for America, to which country he sailed and arrived in safety, about the end of the term of the administration of the elder Adams.

Fresh difficulties now assailed him, as the British government was then claiming her citizens under the alien and sedition laws, and Burk, having become odious to the president through his connection with a gentleman by the name of Smith, who had also incurred his excellency's displeasure, was warned by one of his friends to remove to Virginia, where he would meet with a liberal reception, if he lost no time in removing to that state.[1]

Having fairly escaped these difficulties, he adopted the liberal and enlightened principles of the framers of the American constitution, and entering into the views of the signers of the Declaration of Independence, with that fervor which could be best felt by the down trodden sons of Erin, he commenced in Virginia a semi-political and literary career, which he creditably sustained up to the time of his death.

[1] I have sent you in another envelope a criticism by the president on one of my grandfather's dramas, to which my father has added a note in defense of his parent's memory, as a literary character, which I am happy to see gives some dates and confirms the facts already in my possession.

It was on his way to Virginia, that he met with the widow Curtis (*alias* Christiana Borne) in Boston, whom he afterwards married, and by whom he had one son (my father).

Meeting with a warm reception from the hospitable and chivalrous gentry of Virginia, he adopted that state as his own, and became, heart and soul, an American citizen. Appreciating in a high degree the generosity of the people, who took the houseless wanderer to their hearts and homes, he endeavored to requite their kindness by writing the history of that section of country, whose liberal institutions he had so much reason to admire. I have been told by my father, that much of this history was written on stray pieces of paper, found lying about his writing-desk, on returning from some convivial party, and in like manner many fugitive poems and comedies.

The melancholy circumstances of his duel with M. Cocquebert, I have all in printed form, taken from the *Petersburg Gazette*, Saturday, April 23, 1808, which I will send you, with as much more information as I can gather, as soon as I know that you have received this. I am also in possession of McCreery's *Collection of Irish Music,* in which there are a number of songs by John D. Burk, adapted to the airs therein contained.

Hoping soon to hear from you,

I remain, your most obedient,

JUNIA A. BURK.

John Adams's Critique.

" In the last number of the *Record of the Boston Stage* published in the *Boston Gazette,* allusion is made to Burk's play of *Bunker Hill,* and the following anecdote is related: 'The play of *Bunker Hill* was also performed in New York; President Adams being in the city was invited to attend, and at the conclusion of the piece, he was conducted by the managers and leading actors, to his carriage, with considerable pomp and show. Mr. Barrett, who had acted General Warren, ventured to express the hope, that the president had been pleased. 'Sir,' replied Mr. Adams, 'My friend, General Warren, was a scholar and a gentleman, but your author has made him a bully and a blackguard.' Mr. Adams's critique was at once concise and correct."

The above is a paragraph cut out of a newspaper, entitled *The Dollar Newspaper*, of October 27, 1852, and was productive of the following note by my father (Judge John Junius Burk), inserted in the fly-leaf of a copy of the *Suppressed History of the Administration of John Adams*, by John Wood,[1] in which, by referring to chapter VII, page 162, will be found an explanation of the circumstances, which led to that gentleman's unbiased criticism, and will also throw some light on the information contained in my letter of August 2, 1867.

"Burk 163, *infra*.[2] [A reference to the page

---

[1] Wood at one time edited a paper at Petersburg.

[2] From *The Suppressed History of the Administration of John Adams* (from 1797 to 1801, as printed and suppressed in 1802), by John Wood, author of the *History of Switzerland*, etc., pp. 162–3.

"Dr. James Smith and Mr. Burk of New York, the former a citizen, and the latter an alien, were among the first who were arrested upon the sedition act. They were the editors of a newspaper called *The Time-Piece*, and had inserted a paragraph which did not meet with the approbation of the president." *   *   *   *   *

"Burk knowing, as he was an alien, that he would not only receive the punishment which a federal court would gene-

of Wood's *Suppressed History* in which Burk is
mentioned.] My father, an Irishman, had just
taken refuge in this country, from British despotism in Ireland, *tempore* '98. He, while a
student at Trinity College, Dublin, and a
number of other students, were spectators of an
Irishman, captive in the hands of the British sol-
diery, going to drum-head execution. Burk cried
out on the steps of the college to the other students, loitering there, for any of them, an Irishman, to follow him to the rescue. It was done.
He had to fly for his life, was pursued into a
bookseller's shop, his Irish wolf dog keeping the
constabulary at bay, until, attired in woman's
clothes, he escaped from the back of the house,
and embarked as Miss Daly, a name which
he retained afterwards. The other students,
young men of quality, made their peace with
the government; my father, a poor scholar and
commoner, educated at his uncle's expense, fled.

rally bestow, but be afterwards compelled to leave the
United States, thought it most prudent to take himself off,
without waiting for the issue of a trial. *The Time-Piece*
was, in consequence, dropped, and this being the point which
Mr. Adams wished to accomplish, the trial of Dr. Smith
was never brought forward."

These facts were known to the president, and it was determined to hand Burk over to a British frigate, then lying off Boston, where he would have been hung to the yard-arm. Col. Aaron Burr got wind of the purpose, and notified my father, whose escape he facilitated to Virginia.

The extract from the newspaper — *Adams's critique* on the play — is natural to the man's character, who, however, seemingly a republican in the revolution, reserved the monarchical bias in his heart, and hoped for it in the country. Burk was obliged by his history and the drama, to make Warren speak and act the revolutionary soldier. This, in the estimation of Adams, is acting like "a bully and a blackguard." I have read the play : it is not a deliberate effort of the author, but was thrown off rapidly, upon the requisition of the theatre for a national play, when politics ran high. Besides, it was a matter of course that the president, who had persecuted the author (see page 163) [of Wood's *Suppressed History*] should not value his work. There is a natural consistency between the vulgar criticism of the drama and the ruffianly censorship of the press, by John Adams, who

3

hated liberty, even its real presence in the press."

P. S. If you cannot procure a copy of the work, referred to in my father's note, I am able to supply it, if necessary: also the printed notices of his death, which I would desire to have returned, after inspection.

I remain, sir,

Your most obedient

JUNIA A. BURK.

P. S. I also send you the following letter, which I got my sister to copy from one inserted by my father, on the fly leaf of *McCreery's Songs.* It can be of no other use than, perhaps, as it mentions the names of some other Burks, whom you may know something of.

JUNIA.

From John Burk, Esq.

NACHITOCHES, LOUISIANA, 10th May, 1843.

My Dear Sir,

I feel much pleasure in sending you the lyrics of your able and lamented father. I have learned that my brother Edward, himself a young man of fine poetical and oratorical talents, who died many years ago at Petersburg, Virginia, a few months after his arrival in America, had collected some of the *disjecta membra* of your father's works, and it may be, that William Burk of Richmond knows something about them.

Regretting that I can throw no light upon the biography of a worthy relative of the great Edmund, I remain, dear sir, your faithful friend and servant.

JOHN BURK.

Polar Star and Boston Daily Advertiser.[1]

The publication of a daily paper with this title was begun in Boston, October 6, 1796. The imprint stated that it was printed by Alexander Martin, for the proprietors, but no proprietors were mentioned. The editor was John Burk, a fugitive from Ireland, where he had exposed himself to the vindictive power of

---

[1] From *Buckingham's Reminiscences*, vol. II, pp. 294–300.

the government by his connection with James
Napper Tandy and others. of the band called
United Irishmen.   The first few numbers were
on a crown sheet.   It was then enlarged and
printed on demy; and in about six weeks
appeared on a sheet of royal size.   This, I
believe, was the first attempt to establish a
daily paper in Boston.   The editor's opening
address, and, in fact, all his editorials, indicate
that he was master of a fervid style, and wrote
with feelings intensely opposed to everything
that was hostile to the liberty of speech and
the press.   After expressing his gratitude for
the patronage his paper had received in advance,
and descanting on the advantages of a daily
paper, he proceeded to say :

"This, fellow citizens, is a proof of the advantages arising from a daily publication.   I
call you fellow citizens, for I too am a citizen
of these states.   From the moment a stranger
puts his foot on the soil of America, his fetters
are rent in pieces, and the scales of servitude,
which he had contracted under European ty-
rannies. fall off; he becomes a free man ; and
though civil regulations may refuse him the

immediate exercise of his rights, he is, virtually,
a citizen. He sees a moral, intrepid and enlightened community, ranged under the banners
of equality and justice; and by the natural
sympathy that subsists between the mind and
everything that is amiable, he finds his affections irresistibly attracted; he resigns his prejudices on the threshold of the temple of liberty;
they are melted down in the great crucible of
public opinion. This, I take to be the way in
which all strangers are affected, when they
enter these states; that I am so, will be little
doubted when it is known how much I am
indebted to their munificence and liberality.
I shall give better proofs of it than words:
there is nothing that I would not resign for
your service, but what there is little fear I shall
ever be called on to surrender—my gratitude
and love of liberty."

The election of a successor to President
Washington, was a subject of great interest
at that time. With more modesty than was
exhibited by some foreigners, who had the
control of presses in New York and Philadelphia, Burk refrained from vulgar epithets

and personalities. In this second paper he said :

" Of the election of president we shall say nothing. We have promised impartiality; we will keep our word. From an attachment to public liberty, we hope the future president may be as good a republican as Washington. Never has that venerable patriot been known to utter a sentiment favorable to royalty. The simile of the sublime Longinus may be applied to his resignation; he appears like the sun in his evening declination; though it loses its splendor, it retains its magnitude and pleases more, though it shines less. People of America! with this great example of genius and patriotism before your eyes, you will be without excuse, if you err. Let the man of your choice be a man of talent, information, integrity and republican modesty; a lover not only of your constitution, but of liberty in general. He ought to be a friend of the revolutions of Holland and of France; he ought to be a hater of monarchy, not only on account of the danger, but the absurdity of it; he ought not to be willing to divide the people by any distinctions.

Americans should have but one denomination—
the people."

Burk's feelings were naturally strong against
the British government, and, perhaps, almost as
naturally, in favor of France. " France," he
said, "goes on in the uninterrupted career of
victory. On one side she is employed in regene-
rating the degenerate sons of the old Romans.
In Germany she trails the Austrian eagle in
the dust, while the eye of the directory, like
that of Alexander, is thrown with anxiety for
worlds to conquer. England, under the iron
sway of a profligate administration, exhibits the
melancholy example to nations, of the dangers
resulting from the too great security in the
people. She fights like a desperate gamester,
doubling stakes as she loses. The game is
almost run. The people are generous, brave,
honest and unsuspecting; when they open their
eyes, the delusion vanishes."

Burk's impartiality, at least so far as foreign
politics were involved in controversy, is fairly
illustrated by what follows : "The republic of
America has been scarcely ever placed in so
critical a political situation as at this moment:

her commerce, on one side invaded by a Machia-
velian government, which, in defiance of the
most solemn treaties, continues to take their
vessels and impress their seamen; on the other
side, menaced by a people, who, from the nature
of their government, ought to be, and we hope
still are, the friends of America, but who conceive themselves injured and insulted by the
treaty with England; we hope and believe, that
the men, who voted for and against this treaty,
are alike friendly to the constitution of America
and the liberties of mankind; and we abhor
that gloomy and monastic system of politics,
which condemns to the Inquisition and Bastile,
those who happen to differ in opinion. *The
Polar Star*, like a stern and impartial tribunal
of criticism, shall be open to the reasoning on
both sides; but it will hear only reasoning. It
will curb the spirit of faction; silence the
clamors of revenge; and heal the wounds of
the unfortunate, who have been, or shall be,
under the delusion of error."

In the paper succeeding that in which the
preceding extract appeared, after half a column
of prudent and judicious remarks, upon the

neutrality and impartiality of the *Star*, he says, "Two compositions were sent to the office for insertion, the one 'A Federalist,' the other 'A Patriot of '76.' Both were party pieces. Both were violent. We excluded both." He states that the authors took umbrage at the neglect, and sent impudent letters, one calling him a *royalist*, and the other, a *Jacobin*. He says: "Both lie. One threatens, to attack the editor in the *Chronicle:* the other means he shall be bandied about in the *Centinel*. We probably have done them a service, by refusing them a place in our paper, as they were grossly and shamefully deficient in orthography, etymology, syntax and prosody. Their behavior appears to us the surest proof of the *Star's* impartiality."

In some of the early numbers of the *Star*, Burk published an account of his trial and defence before the board of the University of Dublin, on a charge of deism and republicanism. The writings, which were a cause of this charge, were published in the Dublin *Evening Post*, a paper of great reputation, which strongly advocated the cause of the people against the crown. The agents of the government discovered that

4

he was the author of the pieces, and used their influence with the board to remove him from the university, and he was consequently expelled.

The Polar Star and its editor were not treated with any superfluous degree of courtesy by their Boston contemporaries. Whether this was owing to jealousy of it's engrossing the public favor, or dislike to the intrusion of a foreigner into the pale of American editorship, or from some other cause, is not known. From some of its editorials, it appears, that it was attacked by the *Chronicle, Centinel,* and *Mercury.* In the course of a few weeks the editor published several articles, addressed, " To the editors of the several newspapers in Boston," concerning " the vices that existed in newspaper establishments." He said, " The period of election is ushered in by bickerings, by personalities, by feuds, by heart burnings, by animosity, by contentions and quarrels, which reflect a disgrace on the amiable character of liberty, and are unworthy the literary advocates of a free people."

Perhaps his neighbors did not relish this rebuke—doubtless a very wholesome one—from one, who had just left his native country, to escape the consequences of too much freedom of speech. There is nothing, however, in the editorial columns of the *Star*, which merits a similar rebuke.

Like many other editors—some not unknown at the present day—the publishers of the *Star* boasted frequently of the great amount of public patronage bestowed on their labors. This may sometimes be a successful *finesse* to procure support, but is rather dangerous and hardly an honorable experiment. The *Star* of October 25th, said: " *The Polar Star* has gained by its impartiality, in fourteen days, two hundred and thirteen new subscribers. It has lost two, because it supported the federal constitution, and did not rave in favor of the ridiculous and absurd establishments of royalty and aristocracy; and it has lost one, because, to use the *philosopher's* own elegant language, it is a *milk and water* paper, wants tone, and does not flatter one party more than another. Majority for the *Star* two hundred and ten."

In another paragraph it is said, " A great

philosopher, who inherits the science of Newton, the humanity of Rousseau, and the reasoning powers of Locke, was asked by a gentleman, to subscribe for the *Star*, and refused, *because the editor was an Irishman*."

Burk was evidently chagrined at the silence of the Boston press, in regard to him and his paper. Two months after its first appearance, he said : " Whenever a new paper makes its appearance in Europe, the established papers make honorable mention of their infant brother. They have, at least, the liberality to say: *Such a paper made its appearance on such a day, of such a month, of such a year*. But the sublime sages and politicians, who compile the Boston papers, scorn to imitate such vulgar liberality ; they preserve the most profound and edifying silence on such occasions. If the parents of the *Star* had not been careful to register its birth, regularly, according to the rules of the church, in the temple of liberty, before its godfathers and mothers — the people — it might have died, and its existence been forgotten, before these statesmen would have deigned to notice the existence of such a reptile."

Encouraged by prospects of success and probably by hopes of assistance, the proprietors of the *Star* proposed to publish a semi-weekly paper, in connection with their daily publication, to be entitled : *The Columbian Citizen: a Gazette for the Continent.* But the project was never executed.

Notwithstanding all their self-congratulations and assurances to the public of gratitude for unprecedented favor, they were obliged to call upon their subscribers, for a fulfillment of the conditions of subscription, in order to enable them to keep the *Star above the horizon.* But all was ineffectual. I cannot tell the exact date of its *setting;* but the date of the last I have seen, is February 2, 1797. If this was not the last number, the publication was discontinued in a short time after. and Martin, the printer of it, was engaged in the printing of another newspaper, in Philadelphia.

While in Boston, Burk wrote a tragedy called *The Battle of Bunker Hill, or the Death of General Warren,* which was performed a number of times at the Haymarket theatre. For many years the managers of the Boston theatre used to bring it forward. on special occasions, to gratify the patriotism of the pit and gallery. The tragedy had not a particle of merit. except its brevity. It was written in *blank verse,* if a composition, having no attribute of poetry, could be so called. It was as destitute of plot and distinctness of character, as it was of all claim to poetry.

Burk afterward was the editor of a political paper, in New York, called *The Time-Piece,* and was arrested on a charge of publishing a libel, contrary to the provisions of the sedition law of 1798. The issue of the affair, I never knew. About the year 1800 [1808] it was reported, that he was killed, in a duel, in one of the Southern states.

In the *Richmond Enquirer* of May 27th. 1808, were published " Proposals for publishing by subscription the *Ancient and Modern Music of Ireland,* with original songs, suited to the character, and expressive of its beautiful melodies, which will shortly be issued by John McCreery and Skelton Jones. In the meantime the following essay from the pen of the late John D. Burk, on the Irish music, is given to the public, in order that the lovers of the fine arts, and particularly amateurs in the simple and exquisite expression of almost every tune, which will be admitted into the collection, may judge of the claims of Ireland to the merit of having composed those melodies that breathe the very soul of tenderness itself, or the genuine spirit of hilarity and humor, etc." Then follows an essay of nearly five columns, entitled, *An Historical Essay on the Character and Antiquity of Irish Songs,* by John D. Burk.[1]

In the *Richmond Enquirer* of March, 1808, there appeared an oration, delivered at the new brick church,[2] in Petersburg, on Friday, the

[1] In a biographical sketch of Dr. Thomas Robinson of Petersburg, Va., which was published, not long since, in the *Petersburg Index,* the writer states, " that the preface to McCreery's work was written by Dr. Robinson," and he adds, " it is one of the best dissertations extant on Irish music in so condensed a compass." The writer of this memoir of Dr. Robinson gives it as his opinion, that McCreery's work suggested to the poet Moore, the idea of his *Irish Melodies.* Moore was a fellow student with the doctor, at Trinity College, Dublin. The memoir of Dr. Robinson is anonymous, but was written at the request of Dr. Thomas P. Atkinson, who says that the writer is one who knows of what he affirms. Dr. Robinson was, no doubt, the author of the essay.

[2] It stood where the Court House now stands.

4th of March, 1808, by John D. Burk; about four columns. This oration was delivered five weeks before his death.

In the *Enquirer* of May 6th, of the same year, is to be found an article of nearly the same length, signed B[enjamin] Curtis, giving an account of Burk's duel with M Coquebert, which occurred on the 11th of April, 1808. The article is dated Petersburg, April 23, and is taken from the *Petersbury Republican*, of that date.

Appleton's *Cyclopædia of Biography* contains the following: " Burke, John Doly, author of a *History of Virginia* from .its first settlement to 1804, and of two dramatic pieces, entitled, *Burke's Hill*, and *Bethlem Gabor*. He was a native of Ireland, and first came to America in 1807, where he edited some political newspapers in Boston and New York. He was killed in a duel, by a Frenchman, named Coquebert, in 1808."

The statement that Burk came over to America, in 1807, is erroneous. He came over about ten years previous to that. The mistake may be typographical — perhaps for 1797.[1]

---

[1] He probably came over in 1796.

Burk seems to have had some warm friends. It is said that John Randolph of Roanoke was attached to him. He, it is also said, was a regular and copious contributor to the *Richmond Enquirer.*

Burk's *History of Virginia,* consists of four volumes, octavo. The first three were composed by Burk, himself, and are entitled, *The History of Virginia* from its first settlement to the present day. These three volumes were printed in 1805, at Petersburg, Virginia. Burk, falling in a duel, was prevented from completing the work. The fourth volume was printed by M. W. Dunnavant at Petersburg, in 1816. It is entitled, *The History of Virginia,* commenced by John Burk, and continued by Skelton Jones and Louis Hue Girardin. Only a small part of the volume, sixty-three pages, were written by Mr. Jones, who also fell in a duel. Girardin brings the narrative down to the year 1781.

Advertisement from the Richmond Enquirer, 1816.

The History of Virginia (commenced by Skelton Jones and L. H. Girardin) is now completed and ready for delivery to subscribers.

5

A series of untoward and melancholy circumstances have long delayed the publication of the above work, and its delivery to subscribers. Soon after finishing three volumes of it, Mr. Burk was prematurely and fatally cut off, in the prime of life, and at a moment when his naturally powerful mind had derived additional vigor, from intense and vast researches. Mr. Skelton Jones was then induced to undertake the completion of the task; but he died in the very threshold of that undertaking. Sixty-five pages only have issued from his brilliant pen; and the printing of the part, written by Mr. Girardin, has been retarded by difficulties no less numerous than unexpected.

The portion of the *History of Virginia* which fell to the lot of the last named gentleman, embracing the chief political, civil and military transactions of our great revolutionary period, is, from the very nature of the subject, entitled to national attention. There are in the human constitution, principles, which do not permit us to behold, without a deep and vivid interest, the arduous and glorious struggles, which history often presents to our view. We mean those struggles in which truth contended with error. virtue with profligacy, freedom with tyranny. We feel, even at this distant day, for republican Greece, armed against the invading myriads of Persia; for the United Netherlands resisting the despotism and bigotry of inthralled and inthralling Spain; for the brave and virtuous Swiss. hurling defiance in the face of proud Austria. How powerfully then, must our sympathies be excited. both as men and as citizens. when we see not ancient, nor foreign patriots, but our own beloved and revered forefathers, opposing with successful energy a systematic and wanton infringement of their natural and their chartered rights; creating a new body politic; in short, establishing by their wisdom and cementing with their blood, that political independence and those civil and religious liberties, which we now so happily enjoy; and which, if we continue faithful to our high destinies, no power upon earth, no foreign hostility, no domestic intrigue shall ever wrest from our possession. Surely if the pencil of history has at any time delineated scenes calculated to attract our attention, and engage our sensibilities, such scenes are to be found in the present work. Let us add, that, in the prosecution of this laudable undertaking, the continuator has been guided by a strict and undeviating regard for truth, animated by an indefatigable ardor and research, and by a generous desire of perpetuating to the utmost of his individual exertions, that glorious spirit, those admirable and sacred principles, which dictated the measures and accomplished the exploits recorded in his narrative. He has brought to light a mass of interesting local facts ; detected and rectified errors of mischievous tendency, and all along adapted his style to the inherent grandeur and dignity of his subject. The extracts from his part of the history, already before the public, must, we trust, justify our opinion ; and, indeed, we can produce in favor of the work, a testimonial of much higher authority than ours. Mr. Jefferson's extensive historical collection was kindly opened to the continuator's researches. That distinguished patriot, whose zeal and abilities were so early and so efficiently displayed in those very scenes which Mr. Girardin undertook to retrace, has with his usual affability, condescended to read the manuscript, and bestowed on it his approbation in the following words:

"Thomas Jefferson returns to Mr. Girardin his manuscript, which he has read with great satisfaction. And must express, with sincerity, his peculiar gratification on seeing this portion of American history, that of his native state, so ably recorded for posterity."

Other gentlemen, eminent in the literary world, have spoken in terms equally favorable of those parts of the *continuation,* which have been submitted to their judgment; but we deem it unnecessary to say more on this head. The work is now before the public. Let it be tested by its intrinsic merits.

Conditions.—The whole work is composed in four volumes, of a large octavo size, on fine paper, with a new and handsome type. The fourth volume contains about six hundred pages. The three first volumes fall little short of that quantity.

The original price was to be, to subscribers, three dollars per volume, neatly bound in sheep, and lettered, or two dollars and a half in

boards. The present proprietors have determined to reduce that price half a dollar per
volume, as a small compensation for the una-
voidable delay, which has taken place in pre-
paring and bringing out the last volume.

☞ The above work is deposited for delivery at the bookstore of Mr. Fitzwhylson,
where city subscribers can be supplied; those
in the country will be waited on with it, by an
agent appointed for that purpose.

August 29.

33tf.

Girardin prepared material sufficient for another volume and meditated the publication of
it, but the design appears never to have been
carried into effect. It is somewhat remarkable,
that in his preface to the fourth volume, he
makes no allusion whatever to Jones, as one of the
continuators, although the point of demarkation
between the two, is indicated in a foot note, on
page 63. Mr. Jones edited a paper at Richmond.

A second edition of the first volume was published at Petersburg, in 1822. Printed by
Dickson & Pescud, Bollingbrook street.

From the Catalogue of the Private Library of T. H. Morell, New York, 1866.

74, Burk, John. *The History of Virginia* from its first settlement to the present day. With the Continuation by Skelton Jones and Louis Hue Girardin. Together 4 vols., 8vo. vols. 1, 2 and 3, boards, uncut, rough edges. Vol. 4, sheep. Petersburg, Va., 1804–05–16. Excessively rare.

This is probably the finest copy ever offered for sale. The fourth volume is seldom met with, nearly every copy having been destroyed by fire, and I believe it is conceded to be an established fact, that no copy of this very rare volume exists, in the original boards, every one having been bound.

75, [Burk, John.] The Death of General Montgomery in storming the City of Quebec: a Tragedy. With an Ode in honor of the Pennsylvania Militia, who sustained the Campaign in the depth of Winter, 1777, and repulsed the British Forces from the Bank of the Delaware. Rare. Frontispiece, representing the death of Montgomery, engraved by Norman. 8vo, pp.

81. half morocco. Philadelphia, printed and sold by Robert Bell, 1777.

This is one of the rarest of Mr. Burk's publications, and the only copy I have met with. The plate is very curious, as an early specimen of American engraving.

76. Burk. John. History of the Late War in Ireland, with an Account of the United Irish Association, from the First Meeting in Belfast, to the Landing of the French at Kilala. 8vo. boards, uncut, rough edges. Rare. Philadelphia, 1799.

Curious, as being one of the few writings of John Burk, author of *The History of Virginia*, etc.

In Appleton's *New American Cyclopædia*, vol. IV. pp. 122–3, there is a more accurate account of Burk than that which has been quoted from the *Cyclopædia of Biography* published by the same house, though this also mistakes his name in the same manner as that. "Burke, John Doly, author of one of the best histories of Virginia, born in Ireland, educated in Trinity College, Dublin; was killed in a duel with a

Frenchman near Campbell's bridge, Va., April 12, 1808. He came to this country, in 1797: edited a newspaper at Boston, and, subsequently, another, in New York, where he was arrested, under the sedition law. He afterwards removed to Petersburg, Virginia, where he practiced law and wrote his history. He was the author of a few dramas on historical subjects; one of them was entitled Burk's Hill.

Allen, in his *American Biographical Dictionary*, calls him John Doly Burke, perhaps a typographical mistake for Daly, and says, " he was a native of Ireland and educated at Trinity College, Dublin. Coming to America in 1797, he conducted for a short time a paper at Boston and afterwards at New York, where he was arrested under the sedition law. At the Boston theatre he was made master of ceremonies. He was killed in a duel with Felix Coquebert, a Frenchman, in consequence of a political dispute, April 12, 1808. He published an oration, delivered March 4, 1808.

Dunlop, in his *History of the American Theatre*, appendix, under head of John Burk, gives the

6

following, in the list of American plays and
their authors: Bunker Hill, Joan of Arc,
Death of Montgomery, Fortunes of Argil, Inn-
keeper of Abbeville, Bethlehem Gabor, Female
Patriotism, Which do you like best, the Poor
Man or the Lord?

From Allibone's Dictionary of Authors.

Burk or Burke, John. *The History of Virginia* from its first settlement to the present time;
commenced by John Burk and continued by
Shelton Jones and Louis Hue Girardin, 1804–
1816 : seldom found complete, as almost all the
copies of vol. IV, by Girardin, published in 1816
were accidentally destroyed. Perhaps twenty
or thirty copies of vol. IV may be in existence.

Grahame, the author of the learned and excellent *Colonial History of the United States*, in
a note on page 88, of the first volume, says of
Burk: " *The History of Virginia* has derived
the most valuable and important illustration,
from the industry and genius of this writer.
His style is defaced by florid, meretricious orna-
ment."

Reminiscences of Dr. Thomas Pleasants Atkinson, of
Danville, Virginia, relating to Burk.

John D. Burk was a native of Ireland. who
left his motherland, under the ban of the government, on account of his opposition to its
arbitrary acts and vindictive persecution. He
filled a large share in the public eye, having
written and published. in 1804, three volumes
of *The History of Virginia.* bringing it down to
the breaking out of the American revolution.

Mr. Burk was captain of a Petersburg rifle
company, which he raised, and went with it, to
the seaboard, during the difficulties between the
United States and Great Britain, which followed
the capture of the ship Chesapeake by the
Leopard.

Mr. Burk was high and lofty in his carriage,
haughty in his manners, and imperious and
impulsive in his disposition. He owes his
early and sad death to this last and character-
istic trait. Although haughty in his manners,
strange to say, he exerted great influence over
the young men of his day, literally leading
them captive at his will.

Among his intimate friends in Petersburg, were Thomas Bolling Robertson, afterwards governor of Louisiana, Townsend Stith, brother of Mrs. Robert Bolling of West Hill, John Monro Banister, a son of Colonel John Banister of Battersea, and Roger Atkinson Jones, son of General Roger Jones.[1]

There was then living in Petersburg another Irish refugee, one of the United Irishmen, John McCreery, a scholar and poet of genius. He published many fugitive pieces, among them, The American Star, the rival, in former days of Key's famous Star Spangled Banner. Burk, likewise, published many poetical effusions, mostly songs, his favorite of all which was Burk's Anna, which was on the lips of old and young in those days. He was also author of

---

[1] From another reminiscent it is learned that Burk was a fine looking man, of medium stature; well built, of imposing presence. Coquebert was of middle size, well bred and intelligent. Both associated with the principal families in Petersburg. Burk's most intimate companion was Morris Miller; Daniel Eppes was another associate, and Jack Baker, a lawyer, who was one of the counsel that defended Aaron Burr in 1807. Burk, like a good many other young lawyers of that day, had but little practice in the courts.

several plays written for the Thespian Society
of Petersburg. He sometimes personated his
most important characters, on the boards himself. One of these plays was entitled Bethlem
Gabor.

A copy of the play of Bethlem Gabor, that
formerly belonged to J. D. Burk. is still preserved
by his descendants. It is a duodecimo pamphlet, of about fifty pages, each page averaging
about two hundred and eighty words. The
title is " Bethlem Gabor, Lord of Transylvania,
or The Man-Hating Palatine, an historical
drama, in three acts. By John Burk, Petersburg, printed by J. Dickson, for Somervell &
Conrad. 1807." The pamphlet is covered with
a part of an old play-bill, the play being Sheri-
dan's comedy, The School for Scandal, for the
benefit of Mr. Hopkins, a distinguished comic
actor of that day. The date of performance,
November 12, 1803. The character of Sir Peter
Teazle appears to have been performed by an
actor, named McKenzie.

On the reverse of the title page of this copy
of Bethlem Gabor is a list of the *dramatis
personæ* of the play in print. as acted by profes-

sional actors and in manuscript, as performed by the Petersburg amateur Thespians. The professional actors are arranged as follows: Bethlem Gabor, Mr. Green; Worotzi, Clare; Wallestein, Sandford; Frederick, Hopkins; Lubin, Rutherford: Father Dominick, Comer; St. Leon. McKenzie: Spalatro, Bailey: Cornelia, Mrs. West; Rosalind, West Jr. (Nannette West).

The arrangement of the Thespians was as follows: Bethlem Gabor, J. D. Burk; Worotzi, J. L. Edwards; Frederick, Warrell; Lubin, B. Curtis; Father Dominick, T. Stith; St. Leon. Stainback; Spalatro, L. Edwards.

Some of the parts are not supplied.

On the play-bill cover is written in the handwriting of Burk, "Bethlem Gabor, by J. D. Burk." The autograph signature of B. Curtis is written on the title page and the first page.

The theatre was a small, old, ill looking, wooden building, located between Bollingbrook and Back (now Lombard) street, in the rear of Mr. David Dunlop's lot. Here the actor, Placide, and his company used to figure; and here, the people of the town were often gathered to witness the performance of the Petersburg

Thespians, a company composed of young gentlemen of the town.

Dr. Atkinson, in his boyhood, has seen John Monro Banister, Benjamin Curtis, and others of like standing. taking part in these performances. Besides Burk's play, above mentioned, the doctor remembers another written specially for these Thespians : *Nolens Volens*, or the Biter Bit, by Everard. son of Dr. Isaac Hall, then a resident of Blandford.

Burk appears to have boarded, during the latter years of his life, at the house of a Mrs. Swail, an Irishwoman and a midwife, on Old street, a short distance below the present residence of John E. Lemoine. Esq. It is said, that Burk, while living at Mrs. Swail's. was engaged in writing *The History of Virginia*. His office was on Bollingbrook street, near where the theatre, or Phenix Hall. formerly stood.

Burk's proud. self-willed spirit finally led to his premature death. At the time of the Berlin and Milan decrees, which so excited the public, in 1808, Burk took occasion. on a Sunday, at the table of Powell's tavern, in Petersburg. to denounce the French nation as "all a pack of

rascals." A young Frenchman, named Coquebert, a boarder, being at the table, inquired of
Burk, whether he intended to apply his remarks,
personally, to *him*. Burk replied, "Who are
you, sir? you can interpret what I said as you
like." Coquebert answered, "Very well, sir."
He was a clerk [1] in the store of Messrs. Bells
& McNae. A challenge was accordingly sent
by McNae, one of the firm. Burk's second was
Mr. Richard Thweatt, who had, himself, killed
an antagonist in a duel.

Burk and Coquebert fought, at sunrise, the
next morning (Monday), with pistols, at the
distance of ten paces, on Fleet's hill, beyond
Campbell's bridge, in the county of Chesterfield,
about half a mile from the town. Burk was
shot through the heart at the second fire. He
tore open his waistcoat, jumped up and expired.
Coquebert and his second, mounting horses,
escaped. Neither of them ever returned to
Petersburg. Dr. Atkinson was, at this time,

[1] Captain Charles Kent, who came to Petersburg in 1805,
says that Coquebert was not connected with Bells & McNae,
in business, but was, according to his recollection, a tobacco
agent, engaged in buying tobacco. Another reminiscent,
who knew Coquebert, says that he was not a clerk.

going to school, in Petersburg, to an Englishman, named Davis, author of a rhapsodical sort of romance, of which Pocahontas is the heroine. John Junius Burk, only child of John D., aged about eleven, was a schoolmate of young Atkinson, and had gone home with him in the afternoon of the preceding Friday, to Olive hill, a few miles distant in the county of Chesterfield. Junius Burk was small, but brave and lion-hearted. As the two boys were returning to town on Monday morning, they learned from some countrymen, whom they met near Fleet's hill, that some one had been killed in a duel there that morning, and repairing to the spot, they found the ground wet with blood. The place was in a ravine, some two hundred and fifty yards from the road, in a field on the left hand, in coming to town. It was a piney old field.

The two boys proceeding towards Campbell's bridge, young Burk presently heard that his father had been killed. Young Atkinson, in haste, accompanied his agonized schoolmate to Mrs. Swail's on Old street, where his father's body was laid out. It had been removed from the field in a carriage.

7

The body was borne on the following day (Tuesday), thence to the family burial ground of General Joseph Jones, at Cedar Grove near the town. The funeral procession was the largest ever seen in Petersburg up to that time.[1] Ladies strewed flowers over the grave. No tombstone marks the spot. The grave-yard is near the Mt. Airy work-shops of the Petersburg rail-road.[2] General Jones, belonging to the republican party, was first, postmaster and afterwards collector of the customs, at Petersburg.

John Davis, the teacher above mentioned, was author of *The First Settlers of Virginia,* an historical novel, exhibiting a view of the rise and progress of the colony at Jamestown, a picture of Indian manners, the countenance of the country and its natural productions. A second edition considerably enlarged, 12mo, sheep, was published in New York, 1806. This novel was much ridiculed by the *Edinburgh Review* and others. Davis, in his second edition,

---

[1] Mr. Allen Archer, now an octogenarian citizen of Petersburg, was present at the funeral.

[2] The land now (1868) belongs to Archibald G. McIlwaine, Esq.

published extracts from these notices of his work.

He wrote the following verses in honor of Burk, and they were published at Philadelphia in the *Port Folio*, 1809, p. 77.

Burk's Garden Grave.

John Daly Burk fell in a duel, at Petersburg, Virginia, and lies buried in the garden of General Jones's villa, about a mile from the town.

I climb'd the high hills of the dark Appomattox,
    The stream poured its waters the wild woods among,
All was still, save the dash of the surge from the white rocks,
    Where the sea-fowl indulged in his tremulous song.
On my right, where the poplars with fair branches gleaming,
    Half embosom the high-vaulted villa of Jones,
On the tombstone of Daly the liquid sun streaming,
    Marked the spot, where the bard had found rest for his
        bones.

Oh! rare is the spot, hung with clustering roses,
    Where Virginia's sweet minstrel is gone to his rest,
For the sun's parting ray on his grave oft reposes,
    And the redbreast delights there to build her soft nest.
And oft shall the damsels with bosoms high swelling,
    Whose ruby lips sweetly his soft stanzas sing,
Dejected repair to the bard's narrow dwelling,
    And deck the raised turf with the garlands of spring.

The verses were afterwards republished, with some alterations, in the *Port Folio.* (1814), p. 291, as follows:

MR. OLDSCHOOL:

A very imperfect copy of the following tribute, was published in an early number of the *Port Folio*, under the signature of Atticus. Finding it has become popular, in conformity with Swift's advice, I avow myself its author; and having retouched and enlarged this tributary verse to my lamented friend, I entreat you will do me the honor, to insert it *auctior et emendatior*, in your elegant miscellany.

Burk's Garden Grave. — An Ode.

BY MR. DAVIS.

John Daly Burke, an Irishman by birth, but an American by adoption, fell in a duel with a French gentleman, on the banks of the Appomattox, and was buried in the garden of his faithful friend, the worthy General Jones, a spot which Rousseau would have coveted for the place of his interment, beyond the sepulchres of kings. Burke's *History of Virginia* has "placed

a nation's fame amid the stars;" and his songs
are often warbled by our southern ladies in ·
bower and in hall:

I climb'd the high hills of the dark Appomattox,
  The stream roll'd in silence the wild woods among;
All was still — save the dash of the wave from the white rocks,
  Where the sea-fowl indulg'd his tremulous song.
On my right, where the poplars, in fair clusters gleaming,
  Half embosom the sky-piercing turrets of Jones,
The sun's liquid rays upon Daly's tomb streaming,
    Marked the spot, where the bard had found rest for his
    bones.

Accursed be the hand, with resentment prevailing,
  That pointed the weapon, compelling thy fall;
That brought from their bowers the Muses bewailing,
  Thy body convulsed with the murderous ball.
On the river's stain'd margin, there Clio was seen,
  With Terpsichore mourning thy fine spirit fled;
Thalia no longer retain'd her gay mien,
  But hid in Melpomene's bosom her head.

Yet sweet is the spot, hung with clustering roses,
  Where Erin's lov'd minstrel is gone to his rest;
For the sun's parting beam on his green grave reposes,
  And the wren, sweetly plaintive, builds there her soft nest,
And oft shall the damsels, with bosoms high swelling,
  Whose voices, in concert, his soothing lay sing,
Dejected — repair to the bard's narrow dwelling,
  And deck the rais'd turf with the garlands of spring.

Obituaries of John D. Burk.[1]

FROM A RICHMOND PAPER.

Died at Petersburg, Virginia, on Monday last,
in consequence of a wound, received in a duel,
John D. Burk, Esq.. a native of Ireland, and, for
a number of years last past, a resident of that
place; author of various literary, historical and
periodical works. On the following day his
respected relics were to be interred with military
honors. Those relics once delighted in the en-
dearing domestic virtues, which constitute the
citizen and worthy brother. Liberal and sub-
stantial in his friendship, unsuspicious, open and
generous, he concentrated in his bosom the no-
blest qualities of human nature. He pitied little-
ness, loved goodness, admired greatness, and ever
aspired to its glorious summit! From the native
amiableness of his heart when in the domestic
circle, his humor spread around him cheerful-
ness and gayety, like the refreshing zephyrs of a
summer's evening. Alas! he sleeps in death!

---

[1] These obituaries are preserved in printed form, but without the names of the papers.

" Till mould'ring worlds and trembling systems burst !
When the last trump shall renovate his dust !
Still by the mandate of eternal truth,
His soul will flourish in immortal youth."

Like the thunder-bolt, which rends the majestic oak, death levels its triumphant dart, and virtue and genius wither at the blow.

It is rumored, in this city, that John D. Burk of Petersburg, the author of *The History of Virginia*, fell yesterday morning, in a duel, in that town. At the second fire he fell to rise no more. We fear that this melancholy intelligence is too true. Mr. Burk was a man of a noble and expanded soul, of a rich and splendid genius. His death will leave a blank in the society of Virginia, which years will not fill up.

(The above is too true).

On Tuesday morning last, the remains of John D. Burk were consigned to the grave. He had particularly desired, in his will,[1] that his body should not be interred in a church-yard, and requested, too, that the usual religious formalities on funeral occasions, might be dispensed with.

—

[1] The will contains no such request.

His corpse was, therefore, conveyed to Cedar
Grove, the seat of General Jones. in the suburbs
of the town. and buried with military honors.
The volunteer companies of artillery, cavalry
and infantry attended the funeral. as well as a
numerous concourse of citizens.

The causes, which led to a misunderstanding,
between Mr. Coquebert and the deceased, and
which finally produced so distressing a catastrophe, were of a political nature. In a conversation, at a public table, sometime during the
last week. as we are told, the subject turned
upon the letter of the French minister Champagny, to General Armstrong, lately published :
the deceased expressed himself with considerable
warmth; reprobated the conduct of the French
government towards the United States; and
painted in strong colors the insolence of its
minister. Mr. C. being a native of France,
conceived himself individually assailed, by the
words uttered. as well as insulted by the epithets
applied to his nation and government: he
demanded an explanation of the object of the
speaker. Very few words, however, passed
between Mr. C. and the deceased: the explana-

tion required was not given, and the former, in a few moments, left the room. Soon after a challenge was sent by Mr. C., which was accepted, and early, on Monday morning, the parties, with their seconds, met in a field adjoining town. On the first fire Mr. C.'s pistol snapped and the contents of Mr. B.'s were discharged ineffectually. The second fire proved decisive. Mr. C.'s ball passed through the heart of his antagonist, who expired without a word or a groan. Such is the relation which we have had of the unfortunate affair.

PETERSBURG, *Saturday, April 23,* 1808.

For The Republican.

But should some villain, in support
And zeal for a despairing court,
Placing in craft his confidence,
And making honor a pretence,
To do a deed of deepest shame,
While filthy lucre is his aim;
Should such a wretch with sword or knife
Contrive to practice 'gainst the life
Of one, who, honor'd thro' the land,
For freedom made a glorious stand;
Whose chief, perhaps his only crime,
Is (if plain truth at such a time,
May dare her sentiments to tell),
That he his country lov'd too well:

8

May he — () for a noble curse,
Which might his very marrow pierce!
The general contempt engage
And be the Martin of his age.

                                CHURCHILL.

In all societies, there are men actuated, either
by malice, or envy, to blast the fair fame of
those eminent for their talents or virtues.
Impressions and reports unfavorable to the
character of John D. Burk, have gone abroad
with great facility. Where and in whom these
reports originated, I am unable to say. But I
conceive it my bounden duty, to lay before the
public every circumstance relating to the late
unfortunate duel.

                    " Saturday, April 9.[1]

"Mr. Burk, dining at a public tavern with
his friends around him, expressed his sentiments,
with regard to the French government, in the
following manner:

"What will the cavillers against the administration now say? What will they say to the
letter of Mr. Armstrong, in answer to the arro-

----

[1] From this it appears, that the altercation occurred on
Saturday. The reminiscence, on page 47, making it Sunday, is erroneous.

gant note of Mr. Champagny? I am in hopes, when they read the honest, manly and luminous remarks of an American citizen, in refutation of the pretensions of the French rascals, they will have honesty and modesty enough to withdraw their accusations, and be silent, for the French are all a pack of rascals.

"*Mr. Coquebert.* Did you mean to apply those observations to me?

"*Mr. Burk.* Sir, I do not know who you are; what you are? I did not know there was such a being in existence. Who are you, sir? What are you? I do not so much as know your country, or even your name.

"*Mr. C.* I ask, if you mean to insult me, sir?

"*Mr. B.* Seeing sir, that you have no right to intrude upon my concerns, or conversation, you must even take it as you please.

"*Mr. C.* Very well, sir.

"The observations of Mr. C. were uttered, at the public table, in a tone of defiance which precluded anything like gentlemanly or manly explanation." [1]

---

[1] The foregoing account was given by Mr. Burk himself,

Sunday morning Mr. Burk received the following note:

Sir: I have been so long in the place, that you could not help knowing that I am a Frenchman. I sat so nearly opposite to you, at dinner, that you could not avoid seeing me. What you said, could not fail to hurt my feelings. I do not pretend to control the conversation of any man, inasmuch as it does not relate to me. But I cannot overlook what is said in my very face, let it be said directly, or indirectly. If, (alluding to politics) you did not mean to insult me, and had not observed that a Frenchman was within reach of your words, I suppose you have no objection to ease those feelings, by an acknowledgment of it, in as formal a manner as that I take to address you.[1]

F. COQUEBERT.

Saturday, April 9.

to his friend, that in case the interview proved fatal to him, he should inclose it to me with the correspondence.

[1] It was believed by some, that Burk had for some time evinced a strong dislike to Coquebert.

To the foregoing note Mr. Richard N. Thweatt, the friend of Mr. Burk, delivered the answer, as follows:

Sir: My friend, Mr. Thweatt, who was privy to the conversation you complain of, will arrange with your friend anything necessary to discussion, or battle if it shall be so determined on. I hope you will excuse the inaccuracy of not replying to your polite note by a written answer.

J. D. BURK.

Sunday morning, April 10.

MR. COQUEBERT.

After the preceding notes passed, no farther communication took place between the parties (as I understand), except Mr. Thweatt being called upon to name the time and place for battle.

The fatal event of which is known to the world. The situation, in which I stand, relative to the deceased, will plead my apology to the public, for publishing the cause, which led to the late unhappy catastrophe, together with the consideration of preventing misrepresentations.

B. CURTIS.

April 21, 1808.

Copy of the last Will and Testament of John Daly Burk.

Know all men by these presents, that I, John D. Burk, being now in sound health of body and mind, do give, convey, bequeath and assign, sell and make over all my real and personal estate, together with the proceeds, which shall arise from the publication of my compositions, whether in prose, or verse, unto Townsend Stith, Roger A Jones, and Thos. B. Robertson, their heirs, executors, administrators and assigns, in trust, however, for the payment of my debts, which, if not to be done by the profits of my share in Battersea paper-mills and otherwise, shall be vested in them, absolutely, in the hope, however, that. as men of honor they will accomplish this, and appropriate the remainder according to their best judgment, to my sons, Benjamin Curtis, Henry Curtis, and John Junius Burk; and to this instrument I bind my heirs, executors, and assigns, this 9th day of April, 1808.

JOHN D. BURK.   [Seal.]

And I do farther wish and require, that this conveyance shall be considered as *bona fide* my last will and testament.

JOHN D. BURK. [Seal.]

I wish to annex a codicil to this testamentary bequest, a few observations respecting my youngest son (I mention him only because, from his years, he is most helpless). In my estimation, he possesses all the materials of a scholar, a gentleman and a hero. For the reasons assigned, I recommend him, especially, to the attention of my trustees, executors and friends, and my friends, if my principles were accurately understood, would be the people of Virginia. I might go farther; but I will stop here.

Test.   J. D. BURK.

At a Hustings Court, continued and held for the town of Petersburg, at the Court House of the said town, Tuesday, the 7th day of June, 1808. The last Will and Testament of John D. Burk, deceased, and the codicil thereto annexed, were presented in court, by William Robertson, and there being no witnesses to the said will, Townsend Stith deposed, that he is well acquainted with the hand-writing of the testator and verily believes, that the said will and the signature thereto, are all of the said testator's proper hand-writing: Whereupon the same is ordered to be recorded. And Townsend Stith, one of the executors or trustees named in the said will, refusing to undertake the execution thereon, Tho. B. Robertson, another, being absent from this commonwealth, and the court being satisfied that Roger A. Jones, the other executor, or trustee, will not qualify as such : Therefore, on the motion of John M. Banister (and for reasons appearing to the court), who made oath and together with Theodorick B. Banister, his security, entered into and acknowledged their bond, in the penalty of five thousand dollars, as the law directs certificate is granted him for obtaining letters [of] administration of the estate of the said John D. Burk, deceased, with his said will annexed, in due form.

Attest.   J. GRAMMER, C. T. P.

Will of Elizabeth Swail.

In the name of God Amen: I Elizabeth Swail, of the Town of Petersburg, being weak in body, but of sound and disposing memory. do make and ordain this my last Will and Testament, (hereby revoking all others).

Imprimis. After my just debts are paid, I give the whole of my estate to Junius Burk, Valentine Swail of Telecarner, in the County of Down, in the Kingdom of Great Britain (Ireland) to be equally divided between the said Junius Burk, Valentine Swail. May Leed, and Jane Swail, but if the said Estate cannot be equally divided, unless a sale of the lot takes place, then it is my will and desire that the said lot, lying on Old Street, be sold for that purpose by Benjamin Curtis, whom I do hereby appoint my executor and the proceeds of such sale to be equally divided between the parties aforesaid. All my personal Estate not to be sold, unless in case of a deficiency of funds to discharge my Debts. In witness whereof I have here-unto set my hand and seal, this ninth day

9

of October, one Thousand eight hundred and thirteen.

her
ELIZABETH X SWAIL
mark.

Witnesses,

 her
MARTHA X HEATH
 mark.
MARY THAYER.

At a Quarter session Hustings Court Continued and held, for the Town of Petersburg, at the Court House of the said Town, tuesday, the 2d day of November, 1813.

The last Will and Testament of Elizabeth Swail, decd., was proved, in open Court, by the oaths of Martha Heath and Mary Thayer, the witnesses thereto, and is ordered to be recorded. And, on the motion of Benjamin Curtis, the Executor, therein named, who made oath & together with William Gilmour, his security, entered into and acknowledged their bond, in the penalty of two thousand four hundred dollars, as the law directs. Certificate is granted him, for obtaining a probat of the Said Will, in due form.

 Teste.   J. GRAMMER, C. T. P.

*Notice of Burk's History of Virginia, from the Lynch-
burg Star.*

The first volume of this interesting work has
lately made its appearance here. Than a
correct, regularly digested history of this commonwealth, there was no book more wanted;
and this want by the work before us, as far as it
goes, seems eminently supplied. The historical
sketches extant were imperfect, too succinct, or
disgustingly diffuse, and deficient generally in
point of arrangement and method.

History and biography, at the same time that
they are of all knowledge the most amusing
and interesting, are the most important and
instructive. The world and its concerns, nations
and nature, the sanguinary ravages of ruthless
ambition, and the milder progress of civilization,
science and philosophy, are, by the happy invention of letters and the press, brought into full
review, on the historic page, for our instruction
and delight.

The history of our own country is, of all
others, the most important and interesting.
Pride and self-love impel to this knowledge.
Indeed, the passion seems interwoven with our

very nature, as even the most humble and
obscure thirst to claim origin from some remote
and honorable source.

The work before us is judiciously introduced
by a glance at ancient usage; and by a succinct
view of the political and commercial relations
and posture of Europe, before the discovery of
North America.

The discovery of the country; preparations
for colonization; the dangers, difficulties and
distresses to which the first settlers were exposed,
are recounted with method, animation and sentiment.   The story progresses naturally, and
although indispensably crowded with inference,
quotation and authority, considerable force and
diversity are given to certain incidents and
events, by the masculine, energetic language of
Mr. Burk.

The memorable romantic story of Capt.
Smith; his intrepidity, integrity, sagacity and
miraculous adventures, dangers and delivery,
both in Europe and America; his intercourse
and connection with that independent, arrogant,
yet shrewd and manly son of nature, the savage
emperor, Powhatan, and his very amiable daugh-

ter, the princess Pocahantas (who saved his life at the hazard of her own), will be read and remembered with sympathy and interest, while either taste or patriotism exist in Virginia.

Mr. Burk's marked abhorrence of slavery and usurpation, his ardent adoration of liberty and independence, fire his soul. Thought acquires strength by his pen; nor are bold conceptions frittered.   *   *   *   *Cœtera desunt.*

SKETCH OF THE LIFE AND CHARACTER

OF

JUDGE JOHN JUNIUS BURK.

Obituary.

From a Paper published at Baton Rouge, Louisiana.

DIED.—At the family residence in this city, on Tuesday morning, the 17th inst., Hon. J. J. Burk, a native of Virginia, aged 67 years.[1]

Death of the Hon. John J. Burk.

It is with pain and sorrow, that we are called to record the death of this venerable gentleman. Judge Burk was a native of Virginia, but came to Louisiana, at an early age, making the parish of Iberville, his home and afterwards removing to Baton Rouge, where he continued to reside, almost uninterruptedly, up to the time of his decease.

---

[1] It will be seen, on a subsequent page, that he was ignorant of the date of his birth.

He was possessed of an amiable character, being of a kind, polite and obliging disposition, and always seemed to bear up against the ills of life with that calm, patient and uncomplaining spirit, which marked him the true philosopher.

By profession a lawyer, he became through natural taste and habits of close application to study and research. distinguished for his erudition and knowledge in legal science. He was, moreover, remarkably well versed in classic history, and in the varied branches of polite literature. The science and poetry of ancient Celtic literature and song we remember as a distinctive feature in his partialities and devotion to the more ennobling and refining subjects. with which he had stored his mind. Honest and true in his purposes, with a heart keenly alive to the woes and sufferings of his fellow creatures, he commanded the confidence, love and respect of all who knew him.

For several years he occupied the position of judge. in this judicial district; the duties of which he discharged with zeal and fidelity. If at any time he failed to manifest. in his official or personal relations, that perfection of judgment and wisdom, which is beyond the ken and power of mortals, here below, to reach, it might be said of him, that:

"E'en his failings leaned to virtue's side."

Judge Burk leaves a widow and several offspring, to mourn his loss. He died, at his residence, in this city, on Tuesday morning, the 17th inst., at the ripe old age of sixty-seven.

Green be the memory of the good old man, whose life was gilded by so many sterling though unostentatious virtues; and may Heaven reward his soul with the crowning blessings promised to the pure and upright of earth.

At a meeting of the members of the bar, of the fifth judicial district of Louisiana, held at the Court House of West Baton Rouge, on the 17th of July, 1866, a series of resolutions was passed, in honor of the memory of the Hon. J. J. Burk, late judge of that district, expressing their appreciation of his many virtues, his urbanity of manner, his firmness of character,

his honesty of purpose, as a citizen and a man,
and his sterling integrity as a judge. The Hon.
Reuben T. Posey was chairman of this meeting,
and O. M. Le Blanc, Esq., clerk of the court,
secretary. The proceedings were published in
the Baton Rouge newspapers.

Letter from Miss Junia Burk.

Mr. C. Campbell:

BATON ROUGE, *Oct.* 4, 1867.

Sir:

I received your two letters, the one inclosing
the extracts from my scrap-book, the other
informing me of the return of the book (which
however, I have not yet received): but I have
only at present found time to acknowledge the
receipt of them, my attention having been
wholly engrossed with the care of my then only
remaining parent, who departed this life on the
16th of last month, after a long and severe
illness. Looking over my late mother's papers.
I find the will of John D. Burk: also a play in
pamphlet form, entitled Bethlem Gabor, of which
he is the author. The two sons of the widow
Curtis were Benjamin and Henry. but whom

they respectively married, or what offspring they had, I have no means of ascertaining. As you wish for some particulars concerning my late father, I will endeavor to tell you what I know of his character, and the simple events which marked his life. He told us, that he was ignorant of the date and exact place of his birth, as his mother had been dead some time before the fall of his father, whose premature end, deprived him of the means of ascertaining these facts. He was born in the United States, but whether in Boston (the native place of his mother) or in Richmond, Va., he was totally ignorant.

At his father's death, he was taken in charge by Mr. Thomas Bolling Robertson, then governor of Virginia,[1] and one of the executors of his father's will, and was sent by him to William and Mary College, where he nearly completed his education, being considered a boy of sagacity and integrity, beyond his age; as a proof of which he was allowed to depose as a witness in

---

[1] This is a mistake: he was never governor of Virginia, but subsequently to John D. Burk's death, was governor of Louisiana.

a criminal case at the age of nine. He was
much cherished by his father's friends, who
contrived to fulfil the articles of his last will
and testament, as far as was in their power,
besides giving him free access to the Richmond
theatre, where his father's plays were repre-
sented, and where as he has often told us, he
imbibed much of his love for poetical and historical composition. Being considered a proficient
in the dead languages, and possessing a good
English education, he determined to remain no
longer dependent on his friends, and with this
view came to Louisiana, where he studied law,
and was soon received a member of the bar,
which profession he followed with success, divid-
ing his time, after his marriage, between his
legal studies and the education of his children,
with the added care of a young man, whom he
assumed the charge of educating, under the
same circumstances as those in which he was
befriended by Mr. Robertson. He performed
the journey from Virginia to Louisiana, on foot,
making a digression through the Indian territory,
with the idea of living a free life among the
savages, as he afterwards related to us, when

recounting the eccentric aspirations of a wild but poetical youth.

He was habitually a student and given to literature in its various branches, but he was particularly fond of Irish history and took great pleasure in gathering information of its pristine glory as a country, and its probable future destiny among nations. Like his father, he was both poet and historian, but was distrustful or indifferent concerning the publication of his compositions, and it was only, at the urgent request of his friends, that some of his pieces were published.

As for the events of his life, after he removed to Louisiana, and the date of his death, you find them in the printed obituary, which I sent you, some time since.

He married Margaret Alexandrine Millette, a lady of French extraction, by whom he had thirteen children, only five of whom are now living, four girls and one boy. He also raised and educated Andrew S. Herron, whom he took at the age of twelve, after the death of his father Major Herron of Tennessee, who fell also in a duel; the same young man, whom I mentioned above. now a prominent lawyer of this place, late colonel in the Confederate army, and who has filled the several offices of secretary and attorney general of the state, under the old rule.

I would be happy, if I possessed the talent of narration, in order to note my personal knowledge of my late father, as I knew him. Affection perhaps may bias my appreciation of his private character, but it is also true, owing to his extremely reserved nature, that only those who were in intimate relations with him, could thoroughly know his worth as a private individual. He was a man of the most exalted moral views and unswerving integrity, in his transactions with his fellow men. He was totally incapable of a mean, or little action, and his inculcations to his children and those under his immediate influence, were all of the highest moral tone. I never knew him. from my earliest childhood, to neglect pointing out to the observation of youth the beautiful and true in nature, history and life. His manners were an evidence of his character, though. in their outward demonstrations, savoring of the old style. While pursuing

his avocation of a judge, of this and other
distant parishes, he educated, with the aid of
his wife (herself a former pupil, as he married
her while she was yet very young) and eldest
daughter, four of his younger children, at the
same time keeping open house for the entertain-
ment of his friends and whatever professors of
talent and learning, might be visiting the place
at the time.

I must not neglect to mention, that, for
twenty odd years before his death, he was a
strict vegetarian, although keeping the best of
tables, whilst he was able; he was extremely
abstemious, drinking little or no liquor, and
eating, sparingly, of vegetable food, though he
told us, that in his younger days he was quite
dissipated, but not assigning that as a reason
for his later frugality; on the contrary, he
seemed to have no wish for animal food, and
only drank, rarely, to please his friends.

I am in possession of several anecdotes, related
to me by his friends, which would be irrelevant
here, but which are indicative of his character.
If, later, you should feel any interest in seeing
them, I could supply you with the narration.

I will send you, in another envelope, his likeness, with a copy of J. D. Burk's will, which will authenticate the names of the two Curtises, also my father's.

Begging you to excuse the desultory style of my letter, owing to my increased cares, since the death of my late lamented mother.[1]

I remain, yours respectfully,

J. BURK.

P. S. Accept my sincere thanks for the interest you have shown in the memory of those, so dear to me, also for the tender of the notice of my grandfather, which you propose publish-

---

[1] Judge John Junius Burk was born in the year 1800,* and died July 17, 1866. He married Alexandrine Millette, who was born in the Parish of Assomption, Louisiana, Feb. 4, 1813, and died at Baton Rouge, Sept. 16, 1868. Children of John Junius Burk and Alexandrine, his wife: 1. Norah Mary; 2. Junia (deceased); 3. Junia Mary (deceased); 4. Junia Agnes; 5. Eve Margaret; 6. John Daly (deceased); 7, Robert Emmet; 8, Maria Rosa.

1, Norah Mary Burk married John W. Jones, of South Carolina, Oct. 17, 1850. Children: 1, Patrick Burk (deceased); 2, Dennis; 3, Annie Mary.

* According to this date, he was only about eight years old at the time of his father's death, instead of eleven, as stated in some reminiscences on a former page. The judge was ignorant of the date of his birth, but it was probably in 1800.

ing. I have many friends here, but I prize very highly those, who are connected with the memories of past days, in the Old Dominion.

BATON ROUGE, *Oct.* 13, 1867.

MR. C. CAMPBELL:

Sir: As I promised to give you some anecdotes, illustrative of my father's character, I will do so, although it is with a feeling of diffidence, as to my being able to relate them, and even after having done so, whether they are worthy the relation; but knowing that they are to meet the eye of a friend, I trust them, such as they are, hoping you will forgive the partiality of a daughter, whose affection makes her see all things, connected with her deceased parent, in an interesting point of view.

I give them, as well as I can remember, in the words of those who related them to me.

Anecdotes of Judge John Junius Burk.

Judge Burk was a man of extremely reserved and quiet demeanor, in such a degree, that he was little suspected of possessing the light accomplishments, usually affected by gentlemen, unless accident called forth their demonstration.

11

Being in company with some gentlemen, who were amusing themselves, shooting at a mark, in the grove adjoining his house, it was proposed, by one of the party, to try their skill respectively, at hitting an upright twig, at some yards distant. The proposal seemed, to most of the party, out of the range of probability, when quietly taking the pistol, Mr. Burk aimed at and split the twig, at the first shot.

A short time after, a noisy politician, of opinions conflicting with those of Mr. Burk, becoming displeased at, and taking as a personal affront, some general remarks, published by him, in one of the newspapers, came to town, with the intention of calling him out. One of the shooting party, overhearing him express his intentions towards his supposed enemy, took the occasion simply to remark, that he would prefer, were he in his place, not to have a difficulty with a man whom he had witnessed split a rod, at ten paces, for mere amusement. The gentleman in question ceased his threats and from that time, also, his belligerent intentions.

Mr. Burk had a partiality for smoking a shuck, with a little tobacco enclosed, of which he would consume a quantity, every day, in the form of small cigarettes. A celebrated bully, who kept the faint-hearted of the village in constant awe of his displeasure, chose to make some rude remarks, concerning this peculiarity of Mr. B.'s in his presence and that of several others, directing his observations, pointedly and without mistake, with the intention of intimidating the object of his impertinence; when to the astonishment and terror of all the bystanders (he being much the smaller man of the two) he coolly walked up to him and puffed, several times, the smoke of the offending cigarette, in his face and quietly walked away, without the slightest attempt on the part of the bully, to resent the offence.

On another occasion, attending a term of court, in the parish of Assumption, he gave offence to some of the fire-eaters of the place, by a decision, rendered contrary to their wishes and expectations, when (the interior position and feeble police of the community emboldening them) they determined to take the law in their own hands, and with this intention, armed themselves and waited in the lobby of the Court House, in order to intimidate him, into a compliance with their ideas of justice, as he had not yet set the final seal to his decision. The sheriff, learning of the circumstances, too late to put the parties under arrest, before the judge should enter the court, proposed supplying him with a proper guard, for defence; but this he refused and by the mere quiet and determination, evinced in his demeanor towards them, succeeded in completely disarming the ruffianly intentions of the malcontents, who submitted to the final decision, drawn up on the morning in question, without a murmur.

Embarked on the steamer on a return trip from a term of court, held in the above-named parish, he became aware of the presence of ——, a delinquent who had escaped the justice which would have been awarded to him, in all likelihood, at the previous term of court. in his own parish. Seeing that the recognition was mutual, he came up to Mr. Burk, in private, and asked him if he was not afraid of him: on being answered in the negative, he replied, that he knew he must be much mistaken in his man, if he could admit the possibility of his (the judge's) becoming informer.

On the 27th of February, 1859, the steamer Princess, on her down trip to New Orleans, exploded, causing great loss of life and property. Many honorable members of the bar were on board, on their way down, to plead in the supreme court. Mr. Burk being one of the number (his office as judge having expired some time before), had taken a Latin Tacitus from his pocket, and gone by himself to a snug corner (as he thought) on the guards, in order to peruse his favorite author, when the boat exploded, and (as he afterwards described it) from his comfortable seat on the chair, he found himself on his face, with the clap-boards of the cabin about him. With much presence of mind. he waited a considerable time for the steam to disperse, and then watched his chance for getting off on the stage-plank, which was by this time extended some way into the river, but seeing it crowded by the struggling unfortunate, he preferred trusting to the waves. With this view he pulled off only his coat and swam the space of one-third the breadth of the Mississippi, with his mud-boots on, and arrived safely to shore.

His benevolence was easily excited at the sight of misfortune in any form. On a cold wintry day. seeing a poor woman, wandering about in a forlorn manner, he was struck with her appearance, and inquired the cause of her trouble. On being informed, that she had been turned out of doors, by a cruel landlord, he immediately paid the rent due to the owner of the house and restored her to shelter.

During the late war he spent most of his time, at a small farm, about twenty miles from town, as he preferred living there to remaining within the Federal lines. A Yankee company having occasion to pass that way, one of the party stole his only cloak. Mentioning the circumstance, some time afterwards, in a letter to his family, he wrote. " The rascally Yankees passed here the other night and stole my only cloak, which they might have saved themselves the trouble of doing. Had they asked it, of me, I would have given it, cheerfully, as I have always heard that " the cloak of charity covereth many sins," and God knows they have enough to answer for.

P. S. I enclose, at a later date for your inspection, a passage taken from a work entitled *The History of Ireland,* by the Abbé Mac Geohegan, translated from the French by Patrick O'Kelly. The portion referred to is headed Christian Ireland: the pages 271 and 434.

The substance of the passage referred to, was related to me, verbally, by one father Thomas Burk of St Louis, while speaking to me, concerning our family, of which he said he knew the origin. I have written to him, since I have been corresponding with you, but have not received an answer to my letter. I think he must be dead, as he told me, many years ago, that I must call upon him if I ever want information on this subject.

JUNIA BURK.

The family of Burke, otherwise de Bourk. or
de Burgo, in Ireland, derives its origin from
William Fitz Adelm, one of the first English,
who landed in Ireland under Henry II.   Fitz
Adelm was descended from Serlo, or Harlowen
de Bourgo, son of a Norman lord. named Eus-
tace.   Serlo having espoused Arlotte. mother of
William the Conqueror, passed over with that
prince into England.   Of this marriage of Serlo
with Arlotte, was born Robert, Earl of Cornwall,
from whom descended William. who succeeded
to the dignity of earl.   The latter was father
to Adelm and John. who was father to Hubert
de Burgo,[1] chief justice of England and Earl of
Kent.   He was deprived of his office, judged by
his peers in full parliament, and degraded, for
having counselled King Henry III. to annul the
grand charter and the privileges of his subjects.
Adelm was father to William, known under the
name of William Fitz Adelm: he went with
Henry II to Ireland, who confirmed to him, by
charter, five military fiefs, in a place called Toth.

[1] Cox is not in accordance with Nichols, respecting the
descent of William Fitz Adelm.   We do not mean to recon-
cile them : they may be consulted by the reader.

where the Castle of Canice, at present Castle
Connel, is situated. He then gave him large
estates in Connaught, where the whole family
of the Burkes, his descendants, became settled.
William de Burgo, Earl of Ulster and chief of
that family, having been assassinated, in 1333,
without having any male heirs to succeed to the
possession of his estates in Connaught, two
noblemen of his name and family made themselves masters of all his lands in that pro-
vince and formed two powerful families, distinguished by the name of Mac William Eighter
and Mac William Oughter, a distinction which
continued for a long time. Their houses produced several collateral branches, which gave
origin to many private families.

The sept of Burks was honored with four
peerages, in the persons of Ulysses Burke,
created Earl of Clanricarde, in 1543, by Henry
VIII, Theobald Burk (commonly called Tibbod
ne Lung. that is to say, *the naval*, because he
was conversant in naval pursuits), who was
created Viscount of Mayo, in 1627, by Charles
I, both which titles are still in being.

There have been also two lord barons in

the family. namely. Castle Connel and Britta. These titles do not exist, at present, in Ireland, but are united in the person of N. Burke, captain in an Irish regiment, in the service of his most. Christian Majesty.

Refer to *The History of Ireland*, Ancient and Modern, taken from the most Authentic Records and dedicated to the Irish Brigade. by the Abbé Mac Geoghegan, translated from the French, by Patrick O'Kelly, Esq.. Author of a History of the Irish Rebellion. of 1798. Refer to page 434, same chapter, and you will find several paragraphs—the last referred to, ends in these words: "These writers know how to change the names and signification of actions; they style those, who had betrayed their country, faithful subjects. while those who disdained slavery and chains, and fought valiantly to preserve their freedom, are spoken of, by them. as rebels."

It was from the latter gentry that John Daly Burk claimed to be a descendant.

FINIS.

APPENDIX.

Extract from a letter from Mrs. Ann E. Munford, dated at Richmond, Va., Feb. 9, 1868.

John D. Burk married my grandmother, the widow of Benjamin Curtis, who had two sons, my father, Dr. Henry Curtis of Hanover county, Va., and my uncle, Benjamin, who married a Miss Parsons of Petersburg, and practiced law in that city to the time of his death.

Letter from the same Lady, dated at Richmond, February 21, 1868.

I am sorry not to have it in my power to give you more information of my grandmother, but she died when my father was quite a child.

I have heard from others, that she was an exceedingly elegant, dignified lady, and was particularly remarkable for her beautiful hair, which swept the floor as she sate in her chair. She died at Mr. Hodijah Meade's, in Amelia county, when on her way to the Virginia springs, and was buried in *his* family burying-ground. Uncle Junius Burk lived with my father for some time after his marriage, just before leaving for Louisiana, in which state he married and practiced law, being many years judge and afterwards mayor of the place in which he lived.

He corresponded with my father, occasionally, and there were several letters of his with the papers of my father, which have been lost in the confusion and changes through which we have passed. I have never seen uncle Junius, but know, that he was a very promising young man, exceedingly clever, and have heard my father speak most affectionately of him.

Father had in his possession a manuscript copy of Mr. Burk's songs, which has also been lost, I am sorry to say.

Aunt Curtis, the widow of uncle Benjamin Curtis, would give you the desired information of her husband and children by directing a letter to Mrs. Eliza L. M. Curtis, Scotland Neck, N. C.

The letter you speak of having addressed to my brother [Armistead Curtis] never reached him, I am sure: he left here with his family for Illinois early last summer, where I hope they may do very well. I have only two brothers. him and one other. Tyler, who lives in California. My parents had eleven children, only five of whom are now living.

My father was born in Boston. Mass.. 18th March. 1792: his father left only the two children, my father being the younger.

On the 27th of June, 1813, he married my mother, Christiana Booth Tyler. daughter of Judge John Tyler and Mary Armistead. She died on the

13th of January, 1842. My father died on the 31st of July, 1802. At your request I give the dates from the family Bible.

I am sorry not to know the time of my grandmother's marriage with Mr. Burk, or when they came to Richmond, or went to Petersburg. Aunt Curtis may be able to communicate more satisfactorily. I shall ever regret not asking my father more particularly of many events in his life. In much haste,

Yours respectfully,
ANN MUNFORD.

[When the printing of this work was just about to be completed, there was received from Miss Burk a small dingy pamphlet, containing the following oration.]

An Oration, delivered on the 4th of March, 1803, at the Court House, in Petersburg; to Celebrate the Election of Thomas Jefferson, and the Triumph of Republicanism. By John D. Burk, Attorney at Law.

Friends and Fellow Citizens :

When I consider the magnitude and difficulty of the undertaking, which your partiality has this day devolved on me, an undertaking no less than to celebrate in suitable language, (if indeed any language can reach it) the birth of a World, the regeneration of a great and virtuous people : to pursue with deliberate and luminous step the grand career of the revolution through all its interesting vicissitudes of courage and defeat, of suffering and magnanimity, until the whole is crowned with independence and glory; and afterwards, when this people had lost by infatuation, what they had gained by the sword, to tell how on the fourth of March, 1801, another great victory was atchieved over tyranny by the energies of reason — When I reflect that I ought to take into calculation not merely the visible effects of those grand events on the world as manifested in the improvements in the science of morals and government, but that the imagination enlightened by ardor and the spirit of prophecy, should be sent abroad to rend the curtain, which hides futurity from our view, to calculate their effects on distant posterity, I feel, I acknowledge *my utter incompetence.* In the first instance, the pride of having been thought worthy to execute this task, silenced the suggestions of discretion: but now that the object of this meeting presents itself full on my view, in all its *grandeur* and *sublimity,* I am utterly confounded at my temerity.

I regret that when precision and order are so essential to my subject, I should be so much the slave of emotion: but when I reflect, in the first instance, on the courage, the intelligence, the fortitude, the heroism, the love of country, the contempt of death: when I calculate the combination of virtues which was necessary to arm America against her tyrants: America, a confederacy of colonies badly cemented; England, an empire ancient, vast and consolidated : America, poor and apparently dependant on the mother country for her existence : England, rich and grasping at universal domination : America, an infant in her cradle; England, an *Atlas*, sustaining the world on her shoulders: when I hear the shout of onset, and the shock of battle between nations thus disproportioned in strength, the goodness of whose cause was however in an inverse ratio with their political importance, I am assailed by the *mingled sensation of terror and delight* — I mix with the combatants and share their interest in the battle. And when again I reflect how after his toils and his labours, the American *Samson*, in an hour of fatal security, reclined his awful might in the lap of the *Federal Delilah*, I stand in amaze at the mass of internal vigour, which he must have exerted on the fourth of March to break in sunder the ignominious sleep in which his faculties were steeped and plunged: and that too, just at the moment when the *fatal scissors* were lifted up, and he was about to be shorn of his might by the *deceiver* and *betrayer :* here indeed is a subject for the moral sublime: and cold and insensible must be that heart, which can look on it without emotion.

The discovery of this continent by Columbus, the declaration of Independence in '76, the acknowledgement of Independence by the peace of '82, and the regeneration of the people on the fourth of March, 1801, form together a CONSTELLATION not exceeded in brightness by any in the FIRMAMENT of history.

My discourse then, following the order of events, will naturally divide itself into four heads to equal the number of those epochs.

In my mind, it would be impertinent in any age like this, when the whole moral atmosphere of the world is irradiated with streams of literary glory, to go about to prove to Americans that man has rights which he inherits from nature; rights, for which he stands not indebted to magistrates or kings, but which he received from the great God of the universe in the beginning of things, for the *comfort* for *the security*, of his existence. Amongst those rights, those of primary importance (it is equally unnecessary to specify) are, the right to *life*, to *liberty*, and to *property*. By a strange and (I must say) a monstrous inversion in the order of those terms, the sophistry of tyrants by giving to property, which was the last in the natural order, the first place in the order of language, had virtually defeated man's title to his birth-right: property was every where made the base on which tyrants contrived to erect fabrics of government: property, a circumstance merely accidental, became the site of a fortress from which they were able to overawe and finally to subjugate the earth. Hence the origin of oligarchies, aristocracies, and monarchies, forms, which government assumed according to the caprice of despotism: hence those dynasties of calyphs, of sultans, and of emperors, which grew and flourished by the extinguishment of science and the desolation of the earth. With the exception of the Dutch. Helvetic and Genevan

states: with the exception of two or three republican atoms in Italy, remnants of the freedom of the
middle ages; and, with the exception of that awk-
ward and unbalanced compound of aristocracy,
democracy and monarchy in England, there was
not even the appearance of a free state to be found
upon the earth; and even in those states the little
share of liberty enjoyed by the people, they were
unable to procure but by violent struggles; by years
of war, and oceans of blood. Man every where
groaned in bondage, or poured out his blood in war,
the wicked and blind instrument of power. The
old world, was a spacious prison, every corner of
which was examined with cautious and vigilant
apprehension by tyrants: there was no hope of
escape, no place of refuge, and to aggravate this
various wretchedness, the fruits of the earth destroyed by the ravages of war, or wasted by the
wicked prodigality of courtiers and kings, became
insufficient to feed the growing population.

*Famine, that gaunt skeleton, took her place in the long
and gloomy train of human evils.*

It was at this juncture, when human suffering
was at its height, that the great *Being*, who with his
glance, measures the immensity of space, pointed
out an asylum to his creatures; and Columbus was
charged by the Almighty with the sublime com-
mission of making the *old world acquainted with the
new*. If there be any, who object that Columbus
had no special inspiration from above, but that the
general and immutable laws of creation by giving

to man a fiery energy, a daring spirit of enterprise, were of themselves sufficient to bring about this event, be it so; I am content; the glory of the creator is not diminished by ascribing to his creation an original and essential perfection, which rendered all after interference superfluous.

To Columbus succeeded an host of adventurers, but they were not animated by the same enlarged and benevolent views and intentions — set on by the lust of dominion and the thirst of gold, wherever they touched, ruin and desolation followed: witness the cruelties of the Spaniards in Mexico and Peru, where millions of Indians were sacrificed at the shrine of bigotry and avarice.

It is the good fortune of the people of those states that their fathers were not of the class of mere adventurers: exercised in hardships, and seasoned by misfortunes, they had acquired an habitual hardihood and independence of character, which enabled them to overcome the difficulties of their colonial situation: their own severe afflictions taught them humanity, and their attachment to liberty forbade them to encroach on the rights of others: the lands, which they might have seized by the sword, were procured by purchase, while treaties, on their part. religiously observed, secured to them the confidence and respect of the Indians.

Assembled here from all parts of the old world, they forgot the prejudices, which agitated and divided their several countries: necessity and a sense of common interest drew closer the ties of friendship, and *America became a grand altar of union for the widely dispersed children of men.*

I proceed now to speak of the second grand æra in American history; and in doing this, I cannot forbear noticing another peculiarity, by which the American colonists are distinguished from all others. They always had rights: rights, which they always exercised; which they never relinquished, and the least encroachment on which, on the part of the parent state, they always resisted, always resented. Of this curious fact, the most incredulous, the most prejudiced will be assured by a reference to the history of those colonies: it is there demonstrated that various attempts had been made by Britain previous to the stamp act, and tax on tea, by technical niceties, by forced constructions to fritter away the spirit of charters and of compacts; and that she was in every instance repelled with a spirit becoming the hardy sons of the forest.

If those circumstances be duly considered — the revolution in those states, will be matter of less wonder. It will be regarded as an event necessarily growing out of the temper and habits of the people.

But setting reason aside, with its coldness and precision, and regarding this grand spectacle as it *warmly, forcibly,* as it *sublimely impresses* the senses: what imagination is there so languid, not to contemplate it with *awe:* what heart so cold, so insensible that does not glow with transport, throb with anguish, that does not tremble with expectation, as it successively unfolds its great, its eventful incidents

to the view. In '76 England after a long and glorious war, through the former part of which she had
been conducted by the genius of William Pitt,
found herself in profound peace. She was in the
zenith of her power, and may not inaptly be compared to a *vast colossus, with a foot resting on either
hemisphere, holding in one hand a sceptre of Iron, with
which, under the NAME of GOVRENMENT, she
crushed the inhabitants of IND; while her other hand,
outstretched over those states, scattered, showered down
acts of Parliament, which left the people no alternative
but slavery or resistance: the other nations of the old
world smarting under the lash of recent defeat or awed
by her ascendance, were held in subjection by her glance.*
The spectacle of a tyranny like this, so vast, so imposing, so authoritative, so terrific, so unjust, as might
be naturally expected, filled this continent with
mourning and apprehension: but the people did
not despair: they spake not, they thought not of
submission. By petitions sincere and respectful,
they sought to soften, to touch the heart of their
unnatural parent: by remonstrances, bold, manly,
and argumentative, they laboured to carry to her
reason, conviction of her impolicy, of her injustice:
but tyranny is blind; tyranny is unrelenting. The
petitions and remonstrances were rejected with contempt: the former alternative was again proposed
with renewed harshness and contumely, the only
answer with which Britain condescended to honor
our remonstrance was the *ultima ratio regum.* This,
by the bye, is not the last, only, it is the first, the

last, it is indeed the only reasoning of kings: so much easier is it to ravage a country, and murder its inhabitants than it is to convince them that such conduct is moral or beneficial.

Let us now *pause* — let us imagine what in this eventful, this terrific crisis, was the conduct, the deportment of America — so curiously organized is the human mind that though we all know the event of this contest; although every object we see; although the day, the meeting itself, bring fresh to our minds, numerous, glorious proofs of the result; *we are, notwithstanding, held by a sort of magic, in an agony of suspence, till description has moored safe from quicksands, and storms, the vessel of the state in the haven of Independence.*

The British minister, like Brennus, held in his hand the balance with which he weighed out the terms of submission; and like him too, when remonstrated with on his fraudulent attempt to kick the beam, he replied with the same barbarous brevity "that the only portion of the vanquished was to suffer." Did America bow to the tyranny she despaired of being able to combat; did she coldly calculate the consequences of a contest with a power, compared with whom, in the ordinary scale of computation, she was but an atom; did she attempt to ward off the threatening danger by any compromise inconsistent with her glory?

Had she acted in either of those modes, we had not been assembled here this day to celebrate the anniversary of American happiness, of American regeneration. To God alone is known, what position each of us had occupied in a different order of things; but for myself I will speak without hesitation; had I been an American during this contest, and the result had been different from what it is, could I have found liberty no where else, I had sought it in the woods. I thank God however this case is merely hypothetical : the virtue of our fathers, the vigilance and intelligence of their descendants have happily given us a chance of enjoying liberty in society.

But let us return to the question. How did America act at this juncture? Finding the heart of her tyrant steeled against the voice of nature, and the suggestions of reason, leaving all *inferior tribunals, she solemnly appealed to the God of Battles, and the right hands of her people.*

Then was seen the sublime spectacle of thousands of warriors, with a thousand various weapons, issuing from their forests, or descending like torrents from their mountains, at the call of their country. I see the heroic yeomen in white frocks engaged at Lexington and the British retiring.

There, a mother supports the head of her expiring son; *here*, a maiden hanging over his pale corpse, in speechless agony, weeps for her betrothed — he perished in her sight; but his death was glorious: he died for his country.

My imagination follows the step of freedom to Bunker Hill. Behind a breast-work of earth recently and hastily thrown up, the patriots are posted : — their heads sometimes appear above the parapet — a profound silence reigns amongst them — the British, under cover of a furious cannonade, and animated by military music, ascend the hill with the mechanical step of veteran precision — they now approach the entrenchments — Why do not the Americans fire? Has their courage failed them? Have they concluded on submission? — They are still buried in silence — *But it is the silence of Ætna or Vesuvius, ere they roll their lava on the devoted habitations of men. A flood of fire bursts from every part of the entrenchments. The order of Britain is broken. Her squadrons, as if swept away by whirlwind, disappear.* They rally again, it is true, and take possession of the works relinquished by the patriots : but this battle had all the consequences of a defeat, and *whilst pride is weaving a wreath for her brow, Britannia is watering the sickly leaf with her tears.*

Columbia too weeps for her Warren, who on this hill poured out his blood for his country : but her laurel is freshened by her tears, for they are tears of gratitude and love, and the memory of her *hero* is embalmed in those tears.

Washington now joins the army, and discipline and order follow. The hero stands on the heights of Dorchester — his hand is on his forehead, and he appears planning some enterprise. The American colours carry consternation to the army in Boston ; and the fleet, trembling for its safety, removes to a respectful distance, and finally the town is evacuated, and their boasted armada and their redoubtable army disappear.

The deplorable condition of the Republican army, in the Jerseys, next engages our attention and sympathy.

Those poor fellows, on whose swords hung the fate of liberty, were in want of everything.

Without clothes, and often without food; obliged occasionally to fight and retire before superior numbers, their patriotism, their constancy, did not for a moment desert them. *The rout of this handful of heroes is tracked by the blood, which streamed from their naked and lacerated feet:* the British are close in their rear, and escape appears impossible. The genius of liberty hangs her head, and almost despairs of the Republic.

Trenton, Princetown, Quebec, Saratoga, Cowpens, Yorktown, deathless names! how shall I do justice to your fame. Although my zeal is untired, my time is limited, and I sink under the emotions excited by your glories. I find, however, consolation for my incompetence, by reflecting on your claims to immortality: you have furnished abundant matter for the Painter, the Historian and the Poet: more durable than monuments of brass, or than the Pyramids of Egypt; while those stupendous monuments of human force and human folly shall have long crumbled into dust, your names shall sail forever down the stream of time, ever young, fresh and immortal.

The acknowledgment of independence by the

peace of '82 forms the third grand epoch in American history. This ÆRA had its rise in the love of liberty, which every where prevailed, and in the painful and constant sacrifices of the people. By this event, the principles of eternal justice were consecrated in the hearts of three millions of human beings, while at the same time, a glorious example was held out to the oppressed in every quarter of the globe. Now for the first time, under the mild influence of peace, and in the free and absolute enjoyment of liberty, the natural character began gradually to unfold itself: local prejudices, generated by the division of territory into separate sovereignties, were rapidly giving way to national pride, and to American feelings, while the sciences and those liberal arts, which soften and humanize our nature, but which invariably fly the fetters of the slave and the wild uproar of arms, now ventured to make their appearance in the mild beams of peace. But though independence was atchieved, liberty was not yet in safety; doubts seemed to prevail, of the competence of the old confederation to secure the blessings it had created, and after a long and animated discussion, which nearly divided the people, our present happy constitution was established. The moment this instrument was sanctioned by the votes, of the necessary majority of states, its opponents generously withdrew all opposition, and cheerfully united in giving it effect, and carrying it into operation; but it must not be concealed, that during the debates in convention on

14

the merits of this instrument, opinions of high
aristocratic tendency were artfully introduced by
characters of fortune and influence : and it is equally
clear, that from this constitution we ought to date
the birth of a party, which, though baffled in its
attempts to establish its favorite principles of government in convention, carried those principles with
them into society, and that acting in concert, they
artfully and industriously disseminated their perni-
cious doctrines amongst the people. Thus convert-
ing the confidence reposed in them by reason of
their revolutionary services, into a means of establishing an aristocracy in their own persons, by the
sacrifice of the people on the ruins of the throne.

Observing the profound cunning, the impene-
trable reserve, the daring and at the same time
mysterious projects of the followers of Ignatius
Loyola, they were found acting in all places at the
same moment from the chair of the President, where
like the serpent at the ear of Eve they sat distilling
their poison, through all the offices, where they
contrived to get themselves appointed, down to the
town meeting where they made themselves hoarse
by haranguing in favor of strong government against
equality and anti-federalism. The power of this
party was at this time swelled to an alarming amount
by a host of refugees to whom the magnanimous
moderation of America had afforded an amnesty,
and by swarms of British clerks, factors and agents
with which Britain, who had now again extensively
established her commercial connections, inundated

our seaports. The plans of this party received a momentary check and derangement from the revolution in France: it was a phenomenon, which they contemplated with astonishment; but which they were utterly unable to comprehend: an object so vast, so full of sublimity, so well calculated to excite our sympathy and kindle our enthusiasm by the similarity of its principles to those of our own revolution, and now alas! so well calculated to excite our regret by the reflection that this great people, had only escaped the jaws of the *lion*, to be devoured at last by the *wolf* of usurpation, was not to be openly attacked. The dagger was uplifted; but this was not the moment to strike. They affected to feel the general sentiment of joy on the occasion, in order to give the greater effect to their hostility. The British cabinet, which appeared to be fully sensible of the existence and views of this party, issued orders for seizing American property on the ocean, and the treaty of London, which was the end proposed to herself by England, in those spoliations laid the foundation of our disputes with France, while it at the same time enabled this party, under pretence of guarding against France and of preserving internal quiet, to cloth itself with new and alarming powers. The resignation of the venerable chief, whose genius like a pillar of fire, led us thro' the night of our difficulties, and whose *whole* life was checkered by but one fatal mistake, and the election of a man, who wrote three volumes to prove the superiority of a government composed of nobles and a king, decided the victory in favor of this faction, and the advocates of royalty became the masters of the Republic.

In the commencement of this administration, but a small majority appeared in its favour, and confidence, in the language of metaphor, called with peculiar propriety, a plant of slow growth, was reposed in it with a *sparing* hand and *timid* liberality : but it was a BALL of snow, which grew in its progress, and the peculiar circumstances of the empire just at that moment, with respect to France, enabled them, by addressing themselves to the ruling passion of the people, by alarming their pride and their prejudices, to establish their empire over the hearts of a considerable majority. France, robbing us on the ocean; France, haughtily and contumeliously treating our ambassadors, were ideas of less complexity than the more remote and abstracted consideration of France fighting for liberty against kings; of France, insulted and deceived by the treaty of London : The disposition generally prevailing to believe ourselves in the right, decided the question, and we became true and zealous federalists; but the people at length saw a constant and anxious disposition in the government to enlarge its powers by forced and arbitrary constructions : the attempt at a large military force, the Alien and Sedition laws, with the various prosecutions on the part of the government for libel, gave certainty to those suspicions.

From this moment the mask was laid aside.   The

patience and mystery and cunning by which they had consummated their projects, were exchanged for the *insolence* of triumph and the *arrogance* of tyranny.

They were enraged that the people, whom they foolishly fancied reduced to the lot and satisfied with the condition of slavery, dared to examine their measures.

To detail the various acts of folly and phrenzy, which distinguished this administration from all others, would far transcend the just limits of a discourse like the present: moreover the recital could not fail of *tiring* by its sameness, and disgusting by its folly; some of the acts will never go down to posterity; I instance the case of Luther Baldwin, because the decency and gravity of the historian will not condescend to notice them. It will suffice then on the present occasion, to present a few of the most prominent.

They openly advocated a monarchical form of government.

They dared to threaten the good people of this state, with the disgraceful humiliation of "dust and ashes."

They had the insolence to talk of transporting the republican citizens of Jersey, as though they had been *felons* or *slaves*, within the lines of the invading enemy.

They excluded from office, all the friends to a republican form of government.

They borrowed money at an exorbitant interest in times of profound peace.

They enacted taxes odious and oppressive, for the purpose of defending their tyranny by mercenary soldiers, at a time when the Republic had more than one million of her children able and willing to draw their swords in her defence.

They openly violated the constitution: by an Alien law, which declared war against the growth, population, faith and revenues of the Republic; by a sedition law, which struck at the root of freedom by denying to the people the right to canvass the conduct of their servants.

They sought to plunge us into a war for the purpose of perpetuating their authority.

They packed juries for the purpose of insuring the condemnation of the objects of executive resentment.

They immured in dungeons, the victims of the Sedition law.

But the measure of oppression was full, the delusion of the people at an end: they looked round, and were astonished at their infatuation: the artillery of the press, directed by skilful engineers, thundered against the tottering edifice of Aristocracy, the people lifted their voice and the dome rent in sunder by the shout, tumbled in ruins on the heads of its architects. From this moment a new order of things arose.

The fourth grand Epoch rises to my view in the unclouded majesty of the morning: a sage, long practised in virtue, and whose soul was animated by a larger share of the ætherial fire, was called on to repair the mischiefs which his predecessor had occasioned: Thomas Jefferson, the author of the declaration of Independence, the energetic champion of the moral and physical productions of his country against the precipitate charges of Raynal and Buffon; Thomas Jefferson, whose name associates a boundless range of deep and elegant knowledge, of active benevolence and glowing philanthropy, was chosen to succeed the eulogist of the British form of government: the pretended defender of the American constitutions.

I turn with *disgust* from those times of frantic tyranny to repose my *weary* and *indignant spirit* on characters rich in every great and noble qualification: my imagination hastens with gladness from this dreary and comfortless midnight to sport itself in the solar beam of freedom; to taste the sweetness and fragrance of *Elysium :* The living visions of the poets are embodied in my sight: I feel they are not empty blessings which they had promised us in their immortal songs.

Sacred spirits, who in the midst of dungeons and of chains, attuned your harps in praise of heaven-born liberty, look down on our Republic and rejoice.

The unaffected simplicity and sanctity of primeval manners is realized in the conduct of our governors; our people enjoy the plenty and security of the golden age. The reforming spirit, which has produced those blessings, is still in motion: he treads with the firm step of philosophy in his tour over the earth, *shaking thrones, and electrifying nations.* His step is slow, because he has incessantly to combat the obstinacy of ignorance and the intolerance of superstition ; but he holds on his way in a regular and steady pace, directed by the Torch of science.

Avaunt, then you dull and antiquated Sophists, who pretend to examine the energies of mind by the test of an exploded and unnatural logic; who ridicule the fascinating theories and speculations of genius as the dreams of disease or the vapours of insanity; who attempt to stigmatise the progressive swell and energy of soul by the reproachful epithet of the new philosophy imitating closely in this respect, your predecessors in Physical mistake, who opposed the *vortices* of Descartes and the fallacious analogies of Liebnitz to the solid geometrical conclusions, the rational and sublime harmonies of Newton.

Avaunt — to your schools and your cloisters : *there* shroud yourselves in mystery and mutter your jargon : adore the institutes and science of the dark ages as the most stupendous efforts of human invention, kiss with trembling devotion, the dust of antiquity; abhor the improvements arising from the adventurous spirit of the age, as the works of the evil spirit. To your schools and your cloisters ! *make way* for the children of liberty and science. Let us enjoy the light of the Sun, and the bounty of Heaven : let us pursue, with patient step and adventurous ardor, the secrets of nature well assured, the more intimately we become acquainted with the mysteries of this sublime fabric of our universe, the higher will be raised our admiration and respect for its divine author.

Let us then fellow citizens, on a day like this, dear to freedom and interesting to humanity; let us establish a grand altar of *covenant* and union. I ask you, in the name of the living God, to lay down at this meeting, before we part, those absurd and senseless distinctions of sects, which by interrupting the tranquillity of society, impede the *march* of mind and the progress of civilization.

We are *All Federalists, All Republicans :* let us then break in pieces our idols, and laying our hands with pure and sincere hearts upon the altar, unite in the worship of the *true God.*

We belong to the only portion of society, on the many peopled globe, which enjoys the inestimable privilege of self government: shall we not then unite to preserve this blessing inviolate, and transmit it unimpaired to our children. Alas! Americans, and you, respectable inhabitants of England, of Scotland and of Ireland, who differ with me in opinion, but who are not the less valued by me on that account, what is there in the expensive and soul-depressing system of *royalty* to recommend it to your affections; what in the vain and empty ceremonials of *nobility?* Here, your honest pride and industry are not insulted by the impudent pretensions of privileged classes; no unnatural disqualifications stand in your way to honor and to office;

15

the People here are *every* thing : Princes and Peers, *nothing.*

> Princes and Peers may perish or may fade,
> A breath can make them, as a breath has made,
> But a bold *Yeomanry*, the nation's pride,
> If once destroyed, can never be supplied.

Let us then withdraw our affections from a race of kings and families of nobles to whom we owe nothing; but, who stand indebted to us and to our fathers in a thousand services; let us unite in carrying high as the frailty of mortal circumstances will admit, the destinies of this great country, which adopts us. We are in a vast majority, yet, we ask you in the true spirit of conciliation to unite with us; it will be then matter of little consequence whether it be the intendant at New Orleans, or his most Catholic majesty, or the first Consul of France, that has dared to rob us of a right, which we derive from the letter of treaties and the bounty of nature : as it is, the administration has but to speak, and the haughty despots of Europe however denominated ; Kings, Emperors or Consuls, will be taught a lesson in the American wilderness, which, however mortifying it may be to their pride and their ambition, will be useful to their subjects and the world. Americans, approach this altar : it is the *work* of your own hands : natives of Europe lay your hands on it, it *adopts* and will protect you; fair daughters of America, set the example, truth in its most rugged garb. is respectable, but when it assumes the form of a woman it is irresistible.

Let us hail with acclamations this day of our *safety*, this day of our *union ;* and until the going down of the Sun, let us make the air vocal, and the hills, which overlook our town, respond to the soul exalting sounds of, *Jefferson and Union, Jefferson and Liberty,* unfading be the principles which triumphed on this day, *eternal* be the Republic.

[The following was received after the foregoing had been printed.]

Letter from B. H. Smith, Jr.

Mr. CHARLES CAMPBELL, Petersburg,

Dear Sir: At the request of my aunt, Mrs. Curtis, I write to say, that sickness has prevented her from answering your letter of 28th Feb. She had the misfortune to lose her family Bible, during the late war, and cannot give you the exact day of births and deaths requested.

Her husband, Benj. Curtis, was born Jan., 1790; married Miss E. L. M. Parsons, April 12th, 1810. Edward Tabb Curtis, son of Elizabeth and Benj. Curtis, born March 11th, 1811: died Sept. 14th, 1812. Marion Curtis, daughter of E. L. M. and Benj. Curtis, born Feb. 8th, 1813; died Oct., 1827. Benj. William Curtis, son of E. L. M. and Benj. Curtis, born Oct. 17th, 1816.

Benj. Curtis, husband of E. L. M. Curtis, died Dec., 1819.

Junius Burk, after the death of his father, was adopted by Thomas Bolling Robertson of Petersburg, placed in his father's family, in Richmond; continued there until the marriage of Benj. Curtis with Miss E. L. M. Parsons. He then resided with them, until the death of Mr. Curtis. Mrs. Curtis's brother, Junius Burk, kept a school in Prince George county [Va.], for a short time; was summoned to Louisiana by his former protector, who was governor of Louisiana, Mr. Robertson. After the lapse of a few years, he wrote that he had, married a French girl, out there. Since then Mrs. Curtis has heard nothing from him, until she saw in the papers herein inclosed that he was still living, a judge in Louisiana, residing at Baton Rouge.

My aunt is in such feeble health, that she has forgotten a great deal that would be interesting. She begs to refer to "Moratock;" but I presume the papers have met your eyes ere this.

With much respect, I am yours, &c.,

B. H. SMITH, Jr.

INDEX.